ISHAAN

The Fifth Name of Siva

JOY CHAKRABORTY

ISHAAN

The Fifth Name of Siva

JOY CHAKRABORTY

KALAMOS LITERARY SERVICES LLP

Kalamos Literary Services LLP
Email: info@kalamos.co.in | editorial@kalamos.co.in
First Published in 2023 by

Kalamos Literary Services

ISBN- 978-93-91142-70-4
Copyright © *Joy Chakraborty*(2023)

Ishaan
Joy Chakraborty

Cover Designed & Typeset in Kalamos Literary Services LLP

Print and bound in India.

To Siva.

Karacharana Krtam Vaakkaayajam Karmajam Vaa,
Shravananayanajam Vaa Maanasam Vaaparaadham,
Vihitamavihitam Vaa Sarvametatkshamasva,
Jaya Jaya Karunaabdhe Shri Mahaadeva Shambho

PROLOGUE

I am Ishaan. Ishaan is me. Had I not been Joy, I would certainly have been Ishaan. He is my alter ego. We have both had similar, if not exactly the same experiences. We both indulged in a hedonistic frenzy at a certain time in our lives, faced harrowing circumstances and emerged from those circumstances, victorious and enlightened.

Let me explain. It was towards the end of the month of January 2019. I was, well, how to put it … romantically involved with a young Muslim girl. Things were beginning to heat up. It was a scandal. The folks at home came to know of it and to put a stop to all of these 'misadventures' they intended to lock me away for some time. So I did what any sensible rake would have done. I ran away. I had been a student at Ramakrishna Mission Vidyamandira, Belur Math, where I did my graduation. So I was acquainted with the ways of the *sanyasis* there. I could easily blend into them like a chameleon. So I bought a piece of ochre robe, or *bhagwa*, put it around my body and hopped on a train to Chennai. From Chennai, I went to Kanyakumari. There I worshipped the Virgin Goddess and also a young Tamil girl with flowers. I bent down and touched her feet with my forehead. I was literally begging for forgiveness. I even attempted to swim in the ocean there, as Vivekananda had done. But since I was not Vivekananda, I couldn't do it. I swam a certain distance (towards Sri Lanka), but my right thigh got scratched by the boulders there and it started bleeding. So I got out of the water with the satisfaction that at least I tried to emulate my idol. From Kanyakumari I went to Thiruvananthapuram. There at the Padmanabhaswamy Temple, I stayed for six days. I begged for food whenever I felt hungry, scarcely ever asking for money. What would I do with money when I could simply ask for what I needed? My needs were few. Sometimes, I did beg for money. With it, I went to a cyber cafe, opened my Facebook account and posted my whereabouts on my wall so that the folks back at home would know that I was safe. I had no phone with me. There, near the Temple, I stuck up a friendship with my Malayali mother, whom I call Amma. She is from a well-to-do family and lives in a large house with her husband and my two brothers. She fed me on many occasions. I even shared a lot about myself with her. I intend to meet her soon. From Thiruvananthapuram, I went to Kalady, the birthplace of Adi Shankaracharya. There I bathed in the Periyar river and swam in it. In Kalady, I met my Akka, or elder sister, a young Malayali woman who was living there with her husband, my *jiju*, and two of my young nieces. *Jiju* gave me some money to travel to Coimbatore. I told him about my desire to meet Sadhguru Jaggi Vasudev. I had binged through many of his videos on YouTube and I wanted to meet him. With that money I travelled to Coimbatore. There, a young Maharashtrian man, whom I cannot contact because I have no other information about him, not even his name, came to my aid. He covered all my expenses, taking me to the Isha Foundation at the foot of the Velliangiri mountains. Well, to shorten it up, I couldn't meet Sadhguru. He wasn't available. So instead, I made my way to the Velliangiri mountains. On the way I begged for my food from my

Tamil mother, a poor village woman who had her hut just outside the compound of the Isha Foundation. Amma fed me with all the affection and respect that her vast heart could muster. There were tears of gratitude in my eyes. But I hid them from her. I intend to meet her too, soon enough.

So with the food in my belly, I began climbing Velliangiri. On the way I realized just how difficult it was, especially since I had been a chain smoker. However, I didn't give up. The song '*Dhivara*' from the movie Bahubali played in my mind as I climbed up the mountain. It provided the background score for my adventurous exertions. The song, taken from Jamvuvan's speech to Hanuman in the Valmiki *Ramayana*, essentially means, Siva has upheld; now, Vishnu, nourish! I made it, panting all the way. At the top of Velliangiri, in the dead of the night, at the temperature of one or two degrees Celsius, with nothing on me except for the ochre robe, I had an experience! That experience revolutionized me. That made me a new person. The Joy who climbed down was not the Joy who had climbed up. The older Joy had died there, atop Velliangiri. By now, his corpse has completely rotten away, melting back into Mother Nature. The Joy who has written this story is an altogether new person with a distinctively different take on the world. What was that experience? Well, find it out for yourself. Read it, and yes, do bless me. I need your blessings now more than ever. This book is both a confession and a manifesto. The confession about what I had done, and the manifesto about what I am going to do. With the money that I'll get from the sales of this book, I intend to pay all of those people back who have helped me along my journey. They helped me without even asking my name or whereabouts. That *vada pav* seller at Pune station, that milk vendor near Sabarmati Ashram, that restaurant owner near Kaamakshi Temple. And yes, my Tamil mother still lives near the compound of the Isha Foundation. I have to return the favour. So help me do it.

To top it all up, I'd like to add a poem by Swami Vivekananda. The poem is 'Kali The Mother'. It contains the essence of my story.

KALI THE MOTHER

The stars are blotted out,
The clouds are covering clouds,
It is darkness vibrant, sonant.
In the roaring, whirling wind
Are the souls of a million lunatics
Just loose from the prison-house,
Wrenching trees by the roots,
Sweeping all from the path.
The sea has joined the fray,
And swirls up mountain-waves,
To reach the pitchy sky.
The flash of lurid light
Reveals on every side
A thousand, thousand shades
Of Death begrimed and black —
Scattering plagues and sorrows,
Dancing mad with joy,
Come, Mother, come!
For Terror is Thy name,
Death is in Thy breath,
And every shaking step
Destroys a world for e'er.
Thou "Time", the All-Destroyer!
Come, O Mother, come!

Who dares misery love,
And hug the form of Death,
Dance in Destruction's dance,
To him the Mother comes.

MOOLADHARA

The bed creaked and moaned beneath them and every twitch of their muscles sent a violent shudder down the bed-posts. The raw masculinity of Ishaan was at the very height of its display. He had perfected the art of making love over years of constant and rigorous practice. The family in the room beneath must have sent out dozens of complaints to the hotel reception in the span of this half an hour that he had been having sex with this petite nineteen-year-old Nepali girl. Ishaan had met her barely two hours ago at the lounge of Le Grande, the hotel he had checked into.

He was incredibly good at picking up girls. It was not because of anything he did or said; it was just that young women felt an instant attraction towards him. Maybe it was because of his unkempt appearance. His hair was always a mess and so was his untrimmed beard. There was always an air of aloofness around Ishaan, something which drew women towards him like moths to a flame. But Ishaan thought of nothing else right now, only *her*. *Her* face shimmered in the backdrop of a bright carpet of flowers spread as far as he could see. *She* had a flower in her hands. A plump red rose. *She* loved roses, the bright red ones. Her eyes were like those of a doe, bright and sparkling with life.

He bent forward and took *her* face in his palms … he wanted to kiss *her. She* looked away.

"Ishaaaan!!!" The girl screamed. He looked back at her. She was trembling, beads of sweat trickling down her breasts in the chilly Kathmandu air. He knit his brows together and pounded harder. The girl screamed his name again and again and again, reaching the climax of agony and ecstasy. But he wouldn't blow his load just yet. It had taken him years of practice to perfect this art. Years of constant, rigorous, practice. Finally, after five minutes or so, he let go. He loved the feeling of an orgasm. A chemical soup brewing in the brain, a cocktail of endorphin, dopamine and serotonin. He had learned all of this during his MBBS studies. The brain gets hooked to the 'feel-good' factor of orgasm. It's addictive. The more you orgasm, the more you would want to orgasm. It's nature's way of tricking you into having children so that the process can repeat itself over and over again, ensuring the continuation of the species. But what he really liked about orgasm, was the moment of climax when the mind goes absolutely blank. No memories, no fears, no sorrows. *La Petit Mort.* The little death. He wanted to die, over and over again, just for *her.*

His muscles relaxed and he limped over her body, trying to catch his breath. Both of them were breathing heavily, she more than him. Few moments passed by and the only sound that filled the room apart from them breathing was that of the clock ticking. Tick, tick, tick. It was quarter past midnight. He slid over to her side and reached for the table beside the bed. A half-empty packet of Benson & Hedges welcomed his touch. He deserved one right now he felt after this amount of hard work, this level of performance. He leaned against the bedstead and lit a cigarette. The smoke filled his lungs and seeped into his bloodstream. The blood rushed to his brain. He felt *rewarded.* It's all science, he thought to himself. Smoking and fucking are both basically the same thing. Both make you feel good and both destroy you in the process. He didn't mind getting destroyed, as long as there was pleasure in it. He took a puff, wrapped the smoke around his tongue and blew it at the ceiling. The smoke slowly rose upwards like a coiled-up snake biting its own tail. He looked at his penis. The condom was still on. He pulled off the condom with the fingers of his left hand and flung it carelessly on the green carpet on the floor. The condom fell, splattering all its contents on the carpet … the thick white juice running in all directions.

For I have known them all already, known them all:
Have known the evenings, mornings, afternoons,
I have measured out my life with coffee spoons…

No. Ishaan had measured out his life with upturned condoms. There was a difference. His life without *her* was misery at best. He slept with random girls only to make them feel unwanted and miserable as he himself was. There was a gaping hole at the very centre of his heart, a hole he tried in vain to fill up. All he wanted was to forget the world. A world without *her* was a world without hope, without love and without any purpose. It was a life of decadence and degradation. He had been living this life for some years now and was now beginning to get used to it. The dull haze of sex and intoxication made a comfortable retreat for Ishaan, a retreat from the world where *she* was no longer his. He would cry sometimes at night, only to hear the echoes of his sobs bouncing back from the walls that caged him. He felt caged and shackled by a world where there was no longer love, hope and reason. Only misery paraded along with its entourage of debauchery, eroticism and intoxication. He had nearly given in to this wasteful and decadent life. It was a life not worth living. Yet something in him made him tenaciously hold on to it. Something inside of him always told him to wait, to hold on … because something amazing was about to happen. Something so extraordinary that it would lend an entirely new meaning to his name; it would make him an entirely new man.

He looked at the girl. She was peeping at him with her right eye, the left side of her face buried in the pillow. "What was your name again?" he asked.

The girl only smiled back in response.

He looked back at the ceiling, took another long puff and let the smoke slither up to the top. "Maithili …" He turned towards her, "Yes… Maithili. I think you should go now."

The girl sat up, disheveled and naked. She looked around for her clothes. Her black panty was lying on the floor and her bra was nowhere to be seen.

Ishaan helped her with it by looking under the bed where he found it. He waited for her to dress up, patiently counting the ticks of the clock. It took her full five minutes to dress up completely, without counting the time she took in the bathroom. At last, he grew a tad impatient. "Is there anything else?" he asked her bluntly.

The girl looked at him, surprised. She brushed a lock of hair away from her face and said timidly, "I can't find my purse."

Ishaan looked around for it. He searched the table, the sofa, under the bed, in the bathroom. No, it was nowhere to be seen. "You must have left it at the lounge," he said finally. The girl was mumbling something, but he snapped at her, "How much money did it have?" But he didn't wait for the answer. He bluntly took out a 2000 rupee note, pointing the other end at her.

The girl looked at him for a moment, her eyes betraying disbelief and hurt pride. She felt insulted. She looked at him and said, "It's not the money, Ishaan; my keys are in the purse

A moment of awkward silence passed by, and then Ishaan replied, "Okay, you can sleep here. I'll go to the lounge and look for your purse." That was the best thing to an apology that he could muster.

"No need ..." she replied curtly and left the room in a huff. Just before closing the door, she turned around with a lump in her throat and cried, "We Nepalese women aren't prostitutes ..." and slammed the door behind her.

"Yeah, emotional bitch ...." He mumbled and slumped back on the bed. A bottle of vodka was rolling on the floor near the bed. He picked it up, smelled it and emptied whatever was left inside. Just before falling asleep, his hand touched something under the drawer. It felt hard and rectangular. A purse.

SVADHISTHANA

Bekhayali mein bhi tera hi khayal aye,
Kyun bicharna hai zaroori, yeh sawal aye;
Teri nazdeekiyon ki khushi bemisaal thi,
Hisse mein faasle bhi tere bemisaal aye ....

Ishaan woke up with a start. He looked around in a daze. The music was coming from the table. It was his phone ringing. He sat up on his bed, rubbing both his eyes with the back of his palms. The hangover was terrible. His head was throbbing violently. He ran his fingers over his hair. They had grown down to his shoulders. His beard was unkempt and grizzly. He wrapped the bedsheet around his naked body and staggered over to the table. The music felt like a nuisance at this point. He took the phone and rubbed the moisture off its screen with his thumb. *Mashi.* He took the call.

The voice streamed in from the other side, "Hello, Ishaan …"

"Hyan, bolo, *Mashi* …"

"Were you sleeping? Did I wake you up?" It was a comforting and concerned female voice.

"No, no … tell me …" he replied.

"See, baba, I've seen a pretty little girl for you. She is a *nanad* of Paromita. She lives in Kolkata. Young, beautiful and she is freshly out of NIT. She can sing, sew and even cook a few dishes. You can go see her after you return from Kathmandu."

Ishaan had no clue who this Paromita was, and worst of all he was in no mood to even think of this *nanad* of hers. Marriage was not his cup of tea. So he cut *Mashi* short, "See, *Mashi*, I've told you enough times that I DON'T WANT TO MARRY!" stressing the syllables to make the point clear.

The voice stopped for a moment and then it became tenderer and concerned, "How long will you remain a Devdas, baba? She is not going to come back to you anymore, you know that ..." it paused and then began, "Please, for my sake ... settle down with a good girl and start a family. Give this *Mashi* of yours this bit of comfort at this age. All I want is to see you happy ..." and then it broke into a sob.

Ishaan exhaled; his eyes stuck on a floral painting on the wall. Tulips, daffodils, roses .... Roses. He turned towards the window and walked up to it, dragging the bed sheet along the carpet. He took a long breath again and then said in a calmer voice, "*Mashi* ... *Mashi,* listen to me. Let me return first; then we will talk about this, okay? You don't have to cry ..."

"Will you marry her?" came a faint question full of anticipation.

"We'll see ..." Ishaan replied jocundly.

"When is your flight?"

"Tomorrow."

"Okay. I'll be there at the airport ... and don't forget to bring it. You remember, don't you?"

"Yes, *Mashi,* I remember ... I'll go look for it today in the market."

"White ones."

"Yes, *Mashi*, yes. White orchids. I know," the voice trailed off.

Ishaan looked out the window. The glass panes were embroidered with moist floral patterns. He threw open the latch and pushed the window. The chilly breeze blew through the room. The scent of tobacco and vodka wafted away in the breeze and he was bathed in the cool embrace of the mountain air. He looked at the far away mountains. They were silent, meditative, immersed in eons of contemplation. What wonders could they hold? What repository of wisdom was lying dormant in those distant white folds of rocks and earth in the far, far away horizon? Ishaan longed to be in those mountains and dig out with his very hands those repositories of Life's answers. Life, Ishaan understood, was a long drama of cheating, treachery, loss and pain until the curtain of Death falls on the stage. The shroud of death finishes the drama of life. But those mountains in the distant horizon were eternal, untouched by the vagaries of life. They had kept themselves aloof from the never-ending train of foolishness and deception that Life is, and hence they had escaped death. They were truly immortal in Ishaan's eyes.

He looked at his phone. 10:30 am. The temperature was 20 degrees, sunny weather. The city below beckoned to him with its sights and sounds, like a peddler crying his wares. He could distinctly hear the clatter of vehicles and the chatter of people from his fifth-storey room. Horns bellowed and whistles blew in the mazy avenues of Kathmandu. Le Grande was situated just off Durbar Square. It was just a five minute walk from the hotel. He took a cigarette out from the pack, went to the bathroom, opened the cover of the toilet and sat on the commode. He just sat there with the cigarette dangling down his lips. He didn't light it. He didn't evacuate. He just sat there, with vacant eyes, wrapped up in himself.

Full twenty minutes later, the bell rang. He was suddenly jolted back to his hotel room, the Kathmandu cold, the orchids. He wrapped a towel around his waist and opened the door. The hotel boy stood there with a tray of breakfast and a cup of steaming Darjeeling tea. He was immaculately dressed, topped off with a bow tie. Ishaan let him in.

The boy looked around the room quizzically. The condition of the room was not what it had been when it was given to Ishaan. The furniture was disorganized, the sheets were turned, and even a painting was off its hook, hanging by just one nail. He put the tray on the bedside table, turned to Ishaan and said, half-smiling, "Rough night, sir?"

Ishaan smiled back, "Yeah … rough night."

Just as the boy was about to go, Ishaan checked him, "Hey … wait." He then went to the drawer, bent and took out the purse. "Please give it to the girl … what's the name again… Maithili …" he said, handing the purse over to the boy, "… pretty face, blue skirt …"

The boy looked at him, half-smiling and took the purse from him, "She left the hotel last night in a huff. But I'll contact her, don't worry, sir," he replied quaintly and left.

Ishaan stood there at the door after the boy had gone, closing it slowly, trying to recollect the features of the girl, the scent of her perfume, her voice …. It was a faint recollection. All he could remember was that it was a good night.

Ishaan took a pause. He slowly moved towards the windows and gazed at the mountains in the distant horizon. He kept staring at those mountains, which were immersed in eons of contemplation on the nature of this changeable world. In this world of changing realities and changing relationships, these mountains seemed to be fixed, true and permanent. Where was *she* now? What happened to those spoken and unspoken promises which they had made to each other? All gone. Not a trace left. Ishaan thought about his life without *her*. It was a naked parade of wastefulness. Nothing made any sense. He was sleeping with random girls only to wake up empty inside. Nothing filled that hole in his heart which *she* had made while leaving him. The aching in his heart rose to his lips as a sigh. The mountain breeze blew through his hair in reply.

Ishaan dressed himself up in a bright red pullover and grey corduroy trousers. By the force of habit, while dressing up, he passed his hands over where his *janeu* was. Especially, when there was an overwhelming urge to itch his back, he ardently missed his *janeu*. Thoughts of his *upanayana* streamed in through the cracks of his memory, rusty down the years. Thoughts of his mother, his father, their ancestral home in Kolkata where the ceremony was held, the pond beside the house, that old peepul tree standing next to it … but he checked himself the very next moment and exclaimed, "What the fuck!"

Ishaan didn't believe in all of this casteist mumbo jumbo. In his eyes, there were only two castes; men and women. The rest were all the devious creations of man to oppress his fellow man. He reached for his shoes. Woodland trekkers. He sat on the bed, tied his shoelaces, took out the DSLR from his backpack and took a shot of the room. Yup. His camera was in perfect condition. He hummed a tune and reached for a cigarette. Only two were left in the pack. He would have to buy a new one. He lit it and took out his phone. Forty nine texts on WhatsApp, seventy six Facebook notifications, and three missed calls. Two from *Mashi* and one from Prakash. Prakash Malhotra, his college buddy and now a doctor at a reputable Delhi private hospital. The bastard's wedding is next month. Ishaan is to be the best man; at least that's what Prakash would want him to be. But Ishaan was yet undecided. He zoomed out to the home screen. It was *her*. She was staring at him. The look on her face was *eternal*. She would never age; she would never wither. She would always be the way she was. Ishaan tucked the phone back into his pocket, the left one, took his wallet and briskly left the room.

The streets of Kathmandu greeted Ishaan with a bright, sunny smile. The smiles on the faces of the local Nepali people were always authentic. They were bred in the mountains and grew up in the lap of those mountains. They had grown up to be honest and upright individuals, just like the mountains around them. Their love was authentic and so was their anger. They reflected life faithfully, never taking the aid of deception. Ishaan headed straight for Durbar Square, the hub of Kathmandu. He would chalk out the rest of his itinerary from there. Hanuman Dhoka Durbar Square, the epicenter of the old city, was Ishaan's favourite destination in Kathmandu. Everything was accessible from here. He briskly walked the five minutes to his destination and looked around for a *chaiwala*. There were plenty at Durbar Square. A little boy, of about ten, was standing there with a hand-stitched sweater and a monkey cap, with a kettle in his hand. Ishaan called out to him, "*E, chotu, idhar aa ...*" The boy willingly obeyed. "*Ek kadak chai de.*" The boy poured out some tea into a cup and handed it over to Ishaan. Ishaan took the steaming tea into his hand and handed over a twenty rupee note. The boy was counting the change when Ishaan remarked, "Keep it. Chocolate *kha lena.*" The boy was all smiles. Ishaan took out his camera and clicked a picture of the smiling boy.

Ishaan took the tea which was served in a paper cup and walked towards Durbar Square. He loved the feel of the place. Kathmandu, no matter what anyone said, was truly a cosmopolitan city. You could see people from all corners of the planet walking about in the mazy avenues of the city. There were Americans, there were Britishers, and there were French, German, Japanese, Korean, Chinese and many nationalities of people coming to Kathmandu every day. Some were tourists; some were gamblers trying their luck in the many casinos that covered Kathmandu, and then again some came here for the illegal drug smuggling. And some people like Ishaan came here for sex tourism. People from all around the world, and coming from all shades of life came to Kathmandu for one purpose or another.

A tout caught sight of Ishaan and elbowed his way through the crowd to reach him. "*O Saab ji*, want hotel? Very nice hotel, good price, five hundred only …" the man cried out at two metres distance from Ishaan, still on his way towards him.

Ishaan brushed him aside with a wave of his hand and turned to look at the Palace, or whatever he could make out of it from this distance. The man still came up to him and spoke in a smattering of English and Hindi, "Very nice, very nice, air-conditioned…"

Ishaan cut him short with, "*Itni sardi mein* air condition *se kya karunga, bhaiiya*, I'm already staying at Le Grande. You can go now."

The man paused for a moment and then coming closer said in a lower tone, "Want girl? *Mast ladki*, 20 years, curvy, fair … huh, huh?"

Ishaan lowered his Aviators and said, "Height?"

The man lighted up, "5 '2," he said jocundly.

"And size?" Ishaan quizzed again.

The man looked puzzled, "Which size, sir?"

Ishaan drank up the last dregs of tea in the cup and flung it at a dustbin. He looked at the man and clarified, "*Chut ka ....*"

The man was taken aback. He scratched his head and was about to say something when Ishaan stopped him, "Go and first measure it and then come back. Might not fit ... who knows?" Ishaan left the man there and headed for Basantapur Tower.

The best thing that Ishaan liked about Nepal was that the country had maintained its sovereignty over centuries, unaffected by either the Turkish rulers of India or the Mughal Empire. When all of India bowed down to the might of the Mughals, Nepal stood out as a colossus of defiance and independence. It upheld its culture of Hinduism and Buddhism, while paying great respect to art and architecture. The monuments standing all around Durbar Square bore testimony to the rich and cultured taste of the rulers of this fiercely independent land. Nepal was rich both in philosophy and architecture. The mingling of Buddhist influences with the Hindu tradition of the land had created a wonderful melting pot of culture, art and philosophy. Many scriptures of the Buddhist faith had found ready homes in the libraries of the monarchs of Nepal. Ishaan had read somewhere that many Buddhist monks and scriptures from Bengal found ready shelter under the shadows of the monarchs of Nepal when Bengal was overrun by Muslim rule. Many scriptures from Nalanda found a safe haven in Nepal when its famed library was put to flames by Bakhtiar Khilji. Nepal has always been to India, what Italy has been to Europe. All the wisdom of the past, the scriptures, scrolls and palm leaf manuscripts that contained the essence of Ancient India have found refuge in Nepal. And just like the European Renaissance began in Italy, the Renaissance of India began with great indebtedness to Nepal. Even though the monarchy of Nepal had ceased to exist, the great bonds of friendship that the Indian people share with their Nepali brethren remained unassailed by the twists and turns of global geopolitics. Even though China may want to woo Nepal away from India, the bonds of the past forged over centuries and millennia is too strong to be broken so easily.

When Ishaan reached the Basantapur Tower, he was awestruck by the sheer beauty of the monument. The four storey structure with its peripheral buildings stood like a colossus in the bright concrete square, jutted around by other constructions. It had stood witness to ages of history and would stand for ages to come (granted that another great earthquake didn't strike Kathmandu again). Ratna Malla, Prithvi Narayan Shah and other such glorious names had hallowed Durbar Square with their presence. It was an honour to be there. Ishaan took a picture of the Tower, changed his angle and took another. Then he deleted the first one. A girl was selling fresh flowers under a canopy. He went up to her and asked if he could take a picture of her with the flowers. Ishaan always acted on the dictates of his heart. There was no promiscuity in him going over to the girl for taking her picture. It was a natural innocent impulse to take the picture of a beautiful Nepali girl with some beautiful Nepali flowers. She relented after some hesitation. He took a nice picture of the girl, showed it to her and bought a rose. A bright red rose, and presented it back to her as a gift. The girl smiled, "*Ji*, can you give me that picture?"

Ishaan replied, "Do you have an account on Facebook?"

The girl replied, "Yes."

"Well, send me a friend request; I'll accept it and mail you the picture."

The girl took his account name and blushed.

Ishaan smiled and strode off.

How many pictures of *her* had he taken? Ishaan thought. Innumerable. Those pictures were scattered throughout *her* and his Facebook profiles. These pictures sustained him and made him take the next step in the journey of life. Without those pictures, he would have been dead a long time ago. *Her* memories sustained him, gave him strength and succor, and gave purpose to his existence. Why did he exist? Only to remember *her*, cry over *her*. Remember the chestnut hair, those hazel eyes, those coral lips and that smooth and fair skin? And then he would cry over *her* memories. The memories that had welded his soul to *hers* for eternity, a bond that nothing on earth or heaven could cut asunder. *She* was the very breath of his being.

He fished in his pocket for a cigarette. Nothing. Then he remembered that he had smoked the last one already. He looked around for a cigarette vendor. He was approaching one when suddenly his left pocket started vibrating, then came the music. He took out his phone and looked at it. Prakash. He picked it up.

"Ishaan, *kahan hai tu?* Where are you?" the voice streamed in, orotund and reassuring.

"Still alive, *behenchod.* Why did you call?"

"Just worried, bro. When will you return from your fuckscapade?"

"Tomorrow."

"*Accha,* tell me, how many girls did you do? Five, seven, ten …."

"*Bas do.* Two."

"*Do! Sudhar gaya hai tu* … ha? *Jhoot mat bol.* Don't lie …"

"I'm telling the truth, man …"

"*Accha chor, aa raha hai na tu?* You are coming, right?"

"Hmmm … I'll decide when I meet you next."

"Okay, okay … return safely. Call me when you get off the plane. Okay?"

"*Thik hay, bhai.* Bye."

Ishaan put the phone back in his pocket. He bought a packet of cigarettes from the vendor. Benson & Hedges. His brand. He took one out, put it to his lips and lit it. Smoke. It's all smoke. Smoke, shadows and ashes. The body will turn to smoke. Nothing will be left. Why this strife, all this struggle? All for cheques and cunts. Ishaan laughed. He remembered his first body dissection. Prakash had fainted when Professor Subramaniam ran the blade through the body and the blood sprouted out, red as a rose. So many bodies he had dissected. Life is a lie. The only truth is death. The eternal sleep. Life is but a dream that the dead have. Ishaan paused. He looked up at the sky. His searching eyes spied only the clouds drifting out to meet the mountains, like a lover going to meet his beloved. You will get destroyed, Ishaan thought out to the clouds. The mountains will wring all your life away and pour it out into the oceans. Marriage is an illusion. A fatal illusion. A beautiful lie. Marriage … *Mashi* … Orchids. Ishaan looked at his wristwatch. Casio. 01:00 pm. Have to head to the flower market.

It took Ishaan a full hour to search out the white orchids, in the maze of various other subspecies of orchids, that *Mashi* had asked him to bring for her collection. The taxonomic classification of orchids fascinated *Mashi.* She used to teach Botany at Miranda House. Baba used to teach Physics there. He fell in love with *Mashi* but ended up marrying her twin sister, Ma. Ishaan smelled them. Fresh. The white orchids signify innocence, purity and beauty. Ishaan stumbled through his thoughts. They were his *Mashi's* qualities, not his. He was neck-deep in the muck of guilty pleasures, filthy pleasures. Innocence? Purity?

Morality is the device of the weak to bind the strong down, to stop them from doing what they please. In the state of Nature, might prevailed over right. It was only when civilizations formed that all these conceptions of morality, of divine retribution and all other such bullshit ideas sprang up. Survival of the fittest turned into survival of the shittiest. God? Ishaan smirked. God was invented to guard the weak from the strong.

In the state of Nature, there was nothing such as God. There was only the stronger man and the weaker man. It was the strong, who accomplished great and unimaginable feats. They believed in themselves and that was the reason for their success. It was the strong who procreated and gave birth to their offspring. And it was these offsprings who later eulogized and magnified the deeds of their ancestors and worshipped them as gods. The very idea of God arose out of ancestor worship. The people who run about with words of scriptures in their mouths and try to influence others into worshipping some abstract entity called God are deluded fools. They have thrown the baby with the bathwater. They have forgotten that our gods or God were our ancestors, who had great self-confidence and belief in their abilities, and we as their offspring must have inherited at least an iota of their self-confidence and thus have the power to move the world, without the need for an abstract entity called God. With the blinded leading the blind, tragedy was imminent. The state of things regarding God and religion greatly disturbed Ishaan. Every religious group has its God whom they wish to establish as the supreme Divine entity. The Christians have their God, the Muslims have their Allah and the Hindus have a myriad of gods and goddesses, each claiming supremacy. Of all the gods in the Hindu pantheon, Ishaan had a special fascination for Siva. But Ishaan had a very scientific outlook on Siva. For him

Siva was not a god per se, he was one of those great ancestors of the human race who had accomplished unimaginable feats of greatness in his lifetime and had passed his genes to humanity. For Ishaan, Siva was a shaman, for shamanism was the ancestor of all the religions. He was the shaman par excellence. That Siva is called *Pashupati*, lends credibility to the idea that he communicated with the Spirit of all animals, an idea closely linked to Shamanism. Here was a being, who at the dawn of humanity's existence taught the way of Supreme Self-Realization to one and all. And what was more, he never asked anyone to believe in him. He only asked his disciples to believe in themselves, and tread the path towards Enlightenment. He was an individual endowed with tremendous self-confidence who cared only for the betterment of his fellow humans. That's why we worship him. Not because he is a god, but because he is a human.

Ishaan reached Le Grande at five, drunk and thirsty for more. He headed first to his room to put down his things. The camera. The orchids. His glasses. He then went to the bathroom and turned on the hot water faucet. The steam enveloped the mirror. He rubbed the mirror clean and looked in. The face that greeted him was that of a man in his late twenties, but the eyes … the eyes were those of a dead man. The pensive glance that reflected back from the mirror showed someone who was dying every moment, pining for something … someone who never showed up. Who might never show up. The cup of life is always full, sometimes with pleasure and sometimes with pain. It depends solely on us how we navigate the pain. Ishaan was helpless with loss. The very breath of his being was *her.* Without *her,* nothing seemed to be of any importance. Life was bland without *her* touch. She was to his life, what salt was to food. The air he breathed didn't feel the same without *her*, nor did the water feel as rejuvenating without *her*. Nothing was the same without *her*. Ishaan remembered something. It was a poem that he had read back at school. He had forgotten the poet, but the lines had stuck in his mind …

We look before and after, and pine for what is not
Our sincerest laughter with some pain is fraught
Our sweetest songs are those that sing of saddest thought …

Life, Ishaan understood, is one constant struggle against failure and pain. The pain and injury that Life inflicts on you is perhaps the greatest teacher that there is. No one likes to feel pain, so in order to escape that emotion they revise and recheck their actions, only so that they may avoid pain. But what about the pain that someone's absence causes? There is nothing you can do to stop it. The pain and agony of waking up with a jerk late at night were unbearable, and so was the realization that the pillow beside you, which once used to be occupied, is now empty. The pain caused by loss is perhaps the greatest pain that there is. Physical pain might go away with painkillers but emotional pain is untreatable.

Ishaan looked away from the mirror. He was drunk. He had emptied two bottles of beer at a bar on the way back to the hotel. Now he wanted to have a few shots of vodka. The lounge below was calling him, beckoning him for a drink. Just two shots. He said to himself. Only two shots. And no monkey business tonight, he made himself promise. He had a flight to catch the next morning. KTM-DEL. Nepal Airlines 2051.

MANIPURA

Ishaan eyed his boarding pass rather nonchalantly, as he sat at the airport with his backpack leaning against the seat beside him. The flight had been delayed by an hour. Bad weather. The weather had been fine up until last night, thought Ishaan. It was only in the morning that the sky had drawn upon her face a purdah of moroseness. Like a young bride left behind at her father's house by her husband, the sky was sad. That there was a business afoot, she wouldn't listen to. She wouldn't reason. She would long and long and long. And out of those longing eyes poured out a drop of tear. The first snowfall in years. It was all over the news. The children assembled in droves on the streets to lick the coolness off the air. Ishaan too had felt like a child at first. The powdery snow slowly had begun enveloping the streets with a carpet woven in the clouds. But then he thought of how global warming was fucking up the planet. The erratic weather patterns that this had led to caused much anguish to people all around the globe. Katrina. Amphan. Depleting ozone layer. Increasing sea levels. The world is fucked, and so are we. Nature is a dangerous damsel, not to be played with. She has got teeth hidden deep inside her cunt. Sharp as fangs.

Ishaan sat there engrossed in his thoughts, wrapped up in an aura of aloofness. His mind was divided in two. To marry or not to marry, that is the question. If Prakash and *Mashi* had their way, very soon Ishaan would find himself straddled with a girl he did not love, could not love. He knew all too well that both of them were conspiring behind his back. And Prakash's marriage would provide the perfect opportunity to *Mashi* for broaching the question again, this time with an objective correlative. The proof is in the pudding, she would argue. Look how happy Prakash is now. He is a family man. But did *Mashi* have any ground to argue for the merits of marriage? Did she have a locus standi? She herself had never married. Baba had loved her. But had she ever loved him back? Why else would she give him up for Ma? Women have their secrets, sighed Ishaan. He looked at his watch. 11:23 am. It would be another half an hour or so. Coffee. Ishaan looked around. There was a coffee stall near him. He got up, picked up his backpack and sauntered towards the stall.

The girl at the counter was all smiles, "What can I get for you, sir?"

"I'll have a cappuccino," answered Ishaan.

"Well, take a seat."

Ishaan looked around. Most of the seats were occupied. The stalled flights and the bad weather had caused many to go for a coffee break, it seemed. A blonde woman was sitting in a seat with a kid at her heels. She was feeding the child scraps of food. Burger, perhaps. There was a vacant seat to her left. Ishaan decided to go for it. But two steps into the journey he saw a *Sardar ji* come in and take it up. Ishaan looked for any other vacant seat that he could find. He found one and sat down. He took out his phone. *Mashi* might worry. So he called her up. The phone at the other end rang for a few moments and then came her voice, "Hello?"

"Hello, *Mashi?*"

"Tell me, baba."

"The flight's gonna be late, by an hour or two. You need not come to the airport. I'll do just fine."

"No, baba, I'll come … did you eat your lunch?"

"No, but I'll pop in something, don't worry."

"Okay, okay, eat something first."

"And, *Mashi*, I didn't forget the orchids." Mashi smiled. Ishaan could feel it.

"I love you, baba," came her soft, innocent voice.

Mashi. She was all that he had left now, and he was all that she had left. Ma lived on in her. Their voices were identical too.

"I love you too, *Mashi* …" he said before disconnecting the call.

"Here's your coffee, sir," Ishaan looked up and found a twenty-something girl smiling at him, with a tray of hot cappuccino and complimentary cookies.

Ishaan sat at the café, sipping a hot cappuccino from his mug. The hustle and bustle of the airport around him greatly captivated him. Why were all these people running to and fro? Of course, they had a plane to catch. But what was the incentive for all of their activities? It might be that they were looking forward to going home and meeting their loved ones. Some were on business trips, some on official duty, some tourists just like him, and some just transiting. But what was all this hustle and bustle all about? What would they get on meeting their loved ones, or on finalizing their business deal? Success? Love? What? Ishaan's eyes spied two white men talking to each other in English. One of them was wearing a dhoti and an orange pullover and holding a *japa* bag in his right hand while his left hand held out a Bhagavad Gita. The other man was silently listening to the arguments that the former man was making.

Ishaan could make out what the person holding the Bhagavad Gita was saying. "See … the Bible speaks of God as the Father, but Krishna is the Father, the Son, the Lover, the Husband, the Friend, the Counselor …. He is the complete Incarnation of God. He is the Supreme Personality of Godhead …."

The other man said, "I don't understand the meaning of what you said. In the Bible it is clearly written that God doesn't take a human form. He is abstract and formless. I simply don't buy the argument that God incarnated as a cowherd and played with young girls on the banks of an Indian river; that He stole butter from the villagers and had a good time. Why in a thousand years would God do that …? He is the Monarch of Creation … why would he have the need to steal butter from anyone, everything is His after all…."

The first man said, "I completely understand what you mean, but see here comes the conception of Leela. Krishna had no need to steal butter from anyone … after all, the whole Universe is a dream He is having in Vaikuntha. He stole the butter only to have fun with His Devotees. The Devotees of the Lord are closest to him. And to answer you on whether God has a human form or not, let me ask you, isn't it written in the Bible that Man was created in God's image?"

The other man fumbled, "Yes … but … that is different."

"Yes, or No?" the first man asked.

Finally, after some hesitation, the other man relented and said, "Yes."

"So," the first man began, "if man is created in God's image, then God must be like us, with two hands and two feet, a torso and a head. Krishna is that God. God doesn't need to steal butter; as a matter of fact, he lives in the sea of milk, the *Ksheer Sagara*. It is only his Leela that he came down to Earth and sported with his devotees. He came in his Infinite Compassion for us and he has promised to come again ... this time as Kalki. It's all in this book," he said while holding out the Bhagavad Gita.

The other man took the Bhagavad Gita from him and deftly glanced through the pages. After a while he said, "How much for one?"

"Only five hundred and ninety Nepalese Rupees," the first man replied.

The other man handed over the money, took the Bhagavad Gita and left.

The salesman was left standing. After a while he took out two small cymbals and started singing while playing on the cymbals, "*Hare Krishna Hare Krishna Krishna Krishna Hare Hare, Hare Rama Hare Rama Rama Rama Hare Hare,*" in a loud and sonorous voice.

Ishaan felt like going over to the man and having a chat with him. He finished his coffee, went over to the counter and paid the bill. Then he went toward the man. The man saw him and greeted him with a smile. He then stopped singing and took out another copy of the Bhagavad Gita from his bag.

Ishaan looked at the man and said, "I'll only buy this if you can convince me that Krishna, indeed, is the Supreme God and that there is no one like Him."

The other man looked at him and said, "Are you Hindu? If you are, then you must know that Krishna is the Supreme Personality of Godhead."

Ishaan replied, "I am Hindu ... but I don't believe that Krishna is the ultimate God."

"Have you read the Bhagavad Gita? Then read it. Krishna exclaims to Arjuna:

'… *mattaḥ parataraṁ nānyat kiñchid asti dhanañjaya mayi sarvam idaṁ protaṁ sūtre maṇi-gaṇā iva …*'

Krishna, Himself says that of all the forms of worship, worship to Him is the highest. There is no one higher than Him. He is the Supreme Personality of Godhead."

Ishaan looked him in the eye and said, "You may quote as much from the Bhagavad Gita or the Bhagavad Purana or any other Purana that you wish, but the fact remains that quoting from this scripture or that scripture proves nothing. One tendency with you people is that you always quote from Vaishnava Puranas. If you are really quoting the Puranas, then quote from all Puranas. In the Shaiva Puranas, Siva has been shown as the Supreme Personality of Godhead; why don't you quote from the Shaiva Puranas?"

The other man fell silent. Ishaan went on, "Shaivism is perhaps the most scientific and philosophically sound religion that there is. Siva is the ultimate Yogi, who has destroyed all his base instincts. The imagery of Siva destroying Kama with the fire from his third eye— the eye of knowledge clearly shows that. He is the ultimate; that's why the scriptures, if you are so willing to quote scriptures, mention him as *Ekam Evadwitiyam*, the Unparalleled One, and the One without a Second. From a philosophical point of view, Siva is Purusha while the world is Prakriti. Purusha is always passive while Prakriti is always active. I am not belittling Krishna or Vishnu. As I see it, Siva and Vishnu are the same individuals. He is Purusha. When Purusha wishes to engage with Prakriti, He becomes Vishnu; and when Purusha wishes to disengage with Prakriti, He becomes Siva."

The other man was absolutely silent. Finally, Ishaan said, "Let me have the Bhagavad Gita. You have had enough trouble listening to me. I'll recompense for that trouble by buying this book." Ishaan took the book from him and paid him five hundred and ninety Nepalese Rupees.

The plane rolled into the runway at 12:17 pm. The boarding began another thirty minutes later. The powdery snow had begun peppering the runway with its snowy whiteness. The shroud of snow was slowly enveloping the body of the plane at the same time that the ground workers were busy cleaning it off. The snow had flaked along the edges of the windows of the cockpit and the side windows. Ishaan stood in the queue waiting to board the plane. There was a long queue of people behind him. He could hear a distinct chatter of many different languages as he stood waiting his turn. There were Nepalese, Sindhis, Punjabis, French, British and many more. And there were *Delhiwallahs* like him. Loud, boisterous but loveable. Never ask a *Delhiwallah* who his father is, cause that's what he keeps asking everyone who ever meddles in his business. *"Tu janta hai mera baap kaun hai?"* Ishaan thought of Delhi. His city. Delhi is the 'Dil' of India. No wonder every successive invader tried to force his way into it. From Kurukshetra to Panipat, the last battle, Delhi was the prize. Baba would argue his case for Kolkata, about how it was the cultural hub of India, about how it was the seat of the British Indian Empire. But, and this is a big but ... Kolkata is a recent development. Delhi had been around since the time of the Mahabharata. Even the British had to shift their seat of imperial authority from Kolkata to Delhi at the Durbar of 1911. Anyone who controlled Delhi would control the rest of the sub-continent. Everything about Delhi filled Ishaan with warmth. The winter mornings and the summer evenings. The rains. The wavy waters of the Yamuna. Ma would point to it during the rains and tell him how Vasudeva carried Krishna in a bamboo basket on his head across this very river so many monsoons ago. The gentle grass of the Ramlila maidan … used to sing him to sleep whenever Ma would take him there after school. Ma. The grass and Ma were identical; their touch was equally comforting. Ishaan remembered his first college bunk. His first cigarette. The shade of the Qutub Minar. His first kiss. *Her.*

A gentle nudge to his back broke Ishaan's reverie. He turned around and found a young Nepali girl fiddling with her phone, a leather purse hanging down from the seams of her denim jacket by a strap. The nudge was accidental. The girl looked up at him. Cute.

The hostess ushered Ishaan in with a smile and palms joined in *Namaskar*. Ishaan shook off the cold at the entrance and was received by the warmth of the cabin air. He dusted the flakes of snow off his jacket and took off his Aviators. The dim yellow luminescence of the cabin flooded his vision. People were settling down for the flight. A few turbans here and there, of varied hues. A few blonde heads. An indecipherable chatter of many tongues. Few gesticulations here and there. Laughter. Gossip. Ishaan felt that he had just stepped into the tower of Babel. He waded his way through to 13 E. A seat by the window. Ishaan felt relieved. He tucked his backpack in the cabinet above and settled down in his seat. The orchids were already in the cargo bay. *Mashi* would be pleased. It would be a short flight. One and a half hours. He had to deliver the orchids fresh. The first thing he had to do was go over to *Mashi* and hand the orchids to her. Then he would think of other things, probably head to MyBar with Prakash. Ishaan whistled in satisfaction, thinking of the chilled beer and a drag of *sutta* with Prakash.

"Papa, I want to sit there …"

"No, *beta.* That uncle is sitting there *na* …"

"No, I want to sit there," a little girl was whining, speaking to her father. A *Sardar ji.*

Ishaan looked at them. They had just arrived and were standing by the aisle. The girl looked on expectantly at Ishaan, turning her gaze from him to her father periodically, her head bobbing like a pendulum. The *Sardar ji* smiled apologetically at Ishaan, a faint pink crescent in the bush of his beard. Ishaan smiled back, a crescent in the bush of his beard. Ishaan looked at the girl. Probably ten, with her hair tied up in two plaits reaching down to her shoulders. Her eyes sparkled with the strength of innocence.

He got up, "Okay, sit here."

The girl ran to the window seat, sat up and eyed the runway with sheer excitement. She then looked at Ishaan and said, "Thank you, uncle *ji.*"

Ishaan nodded in approval. Ishaan waited for the *Sardar ji* to slide into the middle seat and then he sat down, at the seat by the aisle. The *Sardar ji* thanked him profusely for his generosity while he was sliding into his seat. Ishaan turned down his thanks with, "It's all right. *Chalta hay.*"

It'll be a short flight, Ishaan said to himself as he settled down in his new seat. There were heads all around. The flight was packed. Two *firangis* sat on seats adjacent to Ishaan's. They were conversing in French. The girl with the purse brushed by him. She may have gone to the toilet. She was wearing a pair of sneakers. Black. Ishaan looked at his watch. 12:34 pm. Any minute now. A few moments later the doors whizzed close. Ishaan quietly buckled his seat belt. The flight hostesses stood on the aisle and did their thing. It was so *ghisa pita* that Ishaan felt like he was in an AIB video. *Is Viman ke do mukhya dwar hay jinse may kud jana chahti hu, kyun ki mere* modelling career *ki bamboo ho gayi hay*

...

Ishaan felt like dozing. He looked at his phone. *She* was smiling at him. Ishaan looked at *her* face intently. Hazel eyes. Dark hair. Bewitching smile. He remembered their first kiss. Under the shade of the Qutub Minar. It tasted like strawberries. That was the flavour of *her* lipstick, or *her* lip balm … he couldn't remember. It had been winter in Delhi. Prakash had lent him his motorcycle. Only for two hours, all right. Or else Dad will murder me. We haven't paid the first installment yet, Prakash had said. *She* rode pillion. The ride was a breeze. He felt like he was in heaven.

Ishaan was suddenly jolted by the acceleration of the airplane. It was taking off. Ishaan brushed his hair backwards with his fingers and put on his earphones. He would play the music after the flight had taken off. After a few moments, everything stabilized. The flight was plying gently through the mountain air. All he could see from the windows were the blue of the sky and tufts of wool-like clouds. Sheep. He would count sheep when falling asleep at his hostel. Ma had taught him to do it whenever he couldn't fall asleep. It had worked like magic. That was one memory of Ma that he cherished. Her lulling him to sleep. Ishaan smiled.

Ishaan tapped open his playlist and played the first song. Penned by Irshad Kamil and crooned by Sachet Tandon, he let it roll over his head …

Bekheyali Mein Bhi
Tera Hi Khayal Aaye
Kyun Bichadna Hai Jaruri
Ye Sawal Aaye
Teri Nazdeekiyon
Ki Khushi Behisab Thi
Hisse Mein Fansle
Bhi Tere Bemisaal Aaye
Main Jo Tumse door hoon

Kyun Door Main rahoon
Tera Guroor hoon
A Tu Fasla Mita
Tu Khwab Sa Mila
Kyun Khwab Tood Doon
Bekheyali Mein Bhi Tera
Hi Khayal Aye
Khun Bicharna Hay Jaroori
Yeh Sawal Aye
Thoda Sa Main Khafa
Ho gaya Apne Aap se
Thoda sa Tujhpe Bhi
Bewajah Ye Malal Aye...

Tears were streaming down Ishaan's cheeks. He was thinking of *her*. The scent of *her* hair. The softness of *her* breasts. The feel of *her* touch. He loved to cry over *her*, and he derived pleasure from it. He was becoming a sadist, and he knew it. But he let the song roll over his head, sink deep into his brain ... gnaw into his memories. *Her* memories. The song played on and he let it lull him to sleep.

He didn't know how long it was. Maybe it had been just fifteen minutes when suddenly he was awoken by a loud thud accompanied by a violent jolt. Ishaan looked around in utter confusion. The plane was shaking violently. People were screaming. The air hostesses were running to and fro on the aisle. He yanked away his earphones and looked around, alert. He looked at the Sardar *ji* next to him and his little daughter. They were terrified. The captain made an announcement. We are experiencing severe turbulence. Kindly follow the safety procedures and all will be fine. Do not panic. I repeat, DO NOT PANIC. But people were panicking all over. The altitude was dropping alarmingly. The oxygen masks popped down from their holders. Ishaan quickly wore his oxygen mask and braced himself. His ear popped in continuous succession. Pop. Pop. Pop. The alarm was ringing in the cabin. The plane was losing altitude fast. He felt the plane nosedive towards the ground. The shouts and screams of the people were unbearable. This WAS DEATH. Ishaan prepared himself for this finality. Images raced down his mind in continuous succession. Bright, detailed images. Prakash. *Mashi*. Ma. Baba. His flat in Delhi. *Her.*

Then it went blank. Absolute nothingness. No thoughts. No dreams. No sorrows. No fears.

He opened his eyes slowly. The light began pouring in through his dilated pupil. Images started forming. At first, everything was hazy … then outlines appeared. The vast blue expanse. The drifting clouds. At first, he could remember nothing. All he could feel was the biting cold and the chilly air blowing through his hair. His head was throbbing violently. He was feeling cold. Terribly cold. All he could see in front of him was the blue depths of the sky. Deep as the ocean. Who was he …? The answer came to him slowly. He was Goblu. No, there was another name … I … Ish … Ishaan. Ishaan Chakravorty. Where was he? He didn't know. There was the sky in front of him … only the sky. He could ask the sky … Ishaan looked around. Snowy mountain peaks were hanging upside down. No … it was not the mountain peaks. It was he who was upside down. Ishaan sat up. He looked around bewildered. Where am I? Then he remembered everything. The plane. The oxygen mask. The images. *Her.* He stood up. He was beginning to panic. All he could see around him were the vast mountains and the litter from the plane. Seats, Masks. Luggage. Broken, burnt shards of metal strewn all around, like litter in Ramlila Maidan after the festivities were over. Where were the people? He looked around himself. He was situated in a dent in the mountains, a place where the mountain had rolled over into a plane area. There was snow all around. Heaps and heaps of snow. The snow must have cushioned his fall. Where was his phone? He madly searched his pockets. He found it in his left pocket. The glass had cracked. How was he alive? He quickly turned it on. There was no network. There was only *her*, smiling at him through the crack in the glass.

Ishaan looked at the horizon. Smoke was billowing at a distance. Maybe that's where the plane had crashed, or most of it had crashed. It may have broken down midair. Who knows? At this point he was ready to believe anything. He ran towards the smoke. The cold was biting. It was digging its fangs deep into Ishaan's flesh. The distant beauty of the mountains which Ishaan had enjoyed from the fifth-floor vantage point of his hotel room faded away by the touch of its harsh reality. The hymen of his blissful wonderings about the mountains was suddenly torn apart by the impact of the harshness of their tough reality. All that engrossed him now was the concern for his safety. He had to find shelter. He had to find some warmth in this biting cold. He ran as fast as he could. He ran.

ANAHATA

Ishaan let out a shrill, suppressed cry of despair and horror as he eyed the wreckage of the airplane at a distance. Burnt shards of metal and litter carpeted his way to the wreckage. The black smoke billowing from it seemed to wave at him, beckoning him for assistance. Where were the people? Ishaan gasped. That little Punjabi girl? Ishaan's eyes welled up. A curious concoction of horror and desperation welled up in his heart. If he was alive, someone else too might be … maybe, that girl too was alive …. Ishaan ran towards the wreckage. The cold wind was blasting him in the face. They felt like daggers of frost. The snow was gaping in. His shoes were sinking in the snow. Ishaan waded his way through the sinking snow to the wreckage. At this distance, the destruction was visible in stark detail. Many seats had completely burnt up. Some were half burnt. And then he saw a body. No, two. A woman was clutching her child. Both of them were charred. Ishaan shrieked. He had seen plenty of bodies, even charred bodies. But this … this was different. This was personal. He looked around in horror. Dead bodies peeked at him from the litter. Some were completely charred. Some were half burnt. Was there no one alive? Then he heard the cry ….

"Someone … anyone … help!" a heavy male firangi voice, punctuated with violent sobs. Probably British.

Ishaan madly ran in the direction of the cry. He ran past the litter. He ran past the snow. He ran past the dead bodies. In this desert of the dead, that voice beckoned to him like an oasis of life. It was hope. Hope that he was not alone. Hope that he'll find company, someone to share the sorrows and the snow with. Hope that he is not having a nightmare. Hope that there's still meaning and purpose. Hope … that there is still Life.

The airplane had broken into two. The section containing the fuselage had completely disintegrated. The burnt shards of metal and the litter were the offspring of its tango with death. What was now left was the hollow cavity of the upper section of the airplane, complete with the cockpit and the seats up to seat section 15; the rest had suffered the calamity. When the airplane had broken down midair, or due to impact with any of the surrounding mountains (Ishaan didn't know which) the gushing air had sucked people and objects from inside the cabin and thrown them away from the doomed flight. Like autumn leaves blown around by the vagaries of the wind, this helpless litter (both people and objects) had been vacuumed out of the airplane and into the surrounding area. Ishaan had been lucky, terribly lucky, to have fallen on a cushion of snow and suffered only a mild concussion. The others … Ishaan didn't know yet.

The cry for help was coming from inside the cavity. Ishaan shouted back, "Wait … I'm coming!" while he was navigating the knee-deep snow that carpeted his way to the wreckage of the cabin.

"O God, O God … thank you," the voice rang out, a curious medley of helplessness and relief. Yup, it was British. Or maybe Australian. Ishaan couldn't pinpoint. A few moments later, as Ishaan clambered into the cabin, the voice asked, "Where are ya, mate?"

Ishaan called back, "I'm here … coming!" The blinding brightness of the snow faded away and there was darkness inside. It took Ishaan a moment to adjust to the darkness of the cabin. Now he saw the owner of the voice. A blond man, probably twenty five, was kneeling paralyzingly helpless in front of a seat. Ishaan rushed to his side. The man was clutching the hands of a woman. Her abdomen had been pierced by a shard of metal. Blood had completely soaked her clothes, and was dripping onto the floor. Red as a rose. The woman was drifting in and out of consciousness. The man looked at Ishaan helplessly, his eyes speaking to him what words failed to convey. Ishaan took a closer look at the wound. He then turned to the man and said, "Get her clothes off."

The man looked at him for a moment. Ishaan yelled back, "Get it off now … I'm a doctor … I can help."

The man instantly obeyed. In a jiff, he pulled off her coat and shirt. She was wearing a pink bra. Ishaan bent over her abdomen. The shard of metal was over five inches long, at least the visible portion of it. He quickly rolled over his sleeves and told the man to clutch her hands tight. "She might scream when I pull the shard out … put something in her mouth … maybe a piece of cloth," Ishaan told the man.

The man quickly tore a piece of his shirt and stuffed it into her mouth.

Ishaan painstakingly pulled the shard out. The woman came to when he had just started tugging at it. She let out a blood-curdling yell, but the sound had been muffled by the cloth. Three inches of metal, all soaked in blood fell to the floor within minutes. The woman's intestines were visible through the wound. Fresh blood poured out. Ishaan turned to the man and said, "Find me some alcohol … quick!"

The man went off. Ishaan looked the woman in the eye. She was helpless with pain. He wiped her forehead with his sleeve and said, "Hold on, lady … hold on a bit longer."

Five minutes later the man returned, a bottle of White Mischief in his hand.

Ishaan quickly poured out some vodka on the wound. The woman yelled again.

The man grasped her hands and cried, "Riley … Riley … hold on, love … I'm here!"

Ishaan looked around for a piece of clean cloth. But he could not find any. Where was his bag? There was gauge in his bag? Ishaan madly searched for his backpack. The woman was in 15C. His seat was in 13E. He went up the aisle. Just at the foot of his seat, he found the little Punjabi girl, a long shard of metal sticking through her back, her hair tied in two plaits, just as it had been before. Ishaan gasped. He ran over to her and turned her over. The shard of metal had gone in through her chest and was sticking through her back, a foot long, painted red with her blood. It was as if she had been a crumb of food stuck between the teeth of Mother Nature, who after a hearty meal, had toothpicked her out of existence. Ishaan's eyes welled up with rage and despair. He yelled out, "Fuck you God!" and fell crying to the floor.

The blond man walked up to him, calling him 'Mate', "What happened, mate?" and he reached down to pick Ishaan up.

Ishaan wiped his tears with his sleeve and said to him, "Nothing … it's just an angel that has gone home …" pointing to the girl.

The man looked at the little dead body for a few moments. Then he turned to Ishaan and said, "She's dead. And you aren't. Get a hang of the truth. There's nothing you can do for her now, mate. But you can still save the life of my wife …"

Ishaan looked at him. His eyes were glistening with tears of gratitude and expectation. Yes, Ishaan said to himself. He was a doctor. It was his business to save lives, and not to pore over those that had no life left in them. Death was an inevitability, Nature's way of signing off a document, no matter how short. She seals life with death. Death will come to us all. But a doctor's business is to delay it. He had to do his business. Ishaan jumped to his feet. He asked the man his name.

"Richard," the man replied.

"Richard, please find me my backpack … blue, with black straps, American Tourister …" he said while using his hands to show the size of the backpack.

The two men madly searched the cabin for it. Finally, Ishaan found it, dangling by just one strap from a broken metal rod at the rear end of the cabin. The backpack had nearly been vacuumed out but had tenaciously held on for its life. There was gauge inside. Ishaan quickly tore up some gauge and applied it to the woman's wound. "Can you find a long piece of clean cloth for me to tie around her belly?" Ishaan asked Richard.

Richard found a muffler and handed it over to him. Ishaan quickly washed it with vodka and tied it around the woman's abdomen, with some extra gauge for the wound. He then turned to Richard and said, "She has lost too much blood … let's see … she'll need to rest."

Richard knelt at the woman's side and kissed her hand. He then turned to Ishaan and said, "Thank you, mate; at least you might just save her life."

Ishaan looked puzzled. "At least!" he gasped.

Richard took a long deep breath and said, without looking up at him, "Yeah … she was pregnant … three months …"

Ishaan immediately looked away. He had lost the courage to look Richard in the face. The blood that was now on his hands was not just the blood of one individual, but two. The other had died without ever knowing what life is. Ishaan felt like throwing up. He was sick to his bones. He ran away from the cabin and into the snow. Just before exiting, he puked.

Ishaan stood outside the cabin, quaking with emotions. A curious concoction of horror, disgust and anguish filled his entire body, emptying his bones of their marrow and filling them with sickness. A half-digested slug of cookies and coffee lay in front of him. He stared at his vomit. The last traces of his intercourse with civilization were quickly seeping into the snow, leaving only a temporary trace of brown. "Is this really happening to me?" Ishaan said to himself. All his plans were dissolving into the snow with the vomit. *Mashi*. The orchids. Prakash. MyBar. Chilled beer. *Sutta*. Ishaan breathed. The vapour rose up into the air, slowly drifting upwards to meet the sky. His vapour was like a little stream that was wending its way upwards to meet the concourse of clouds in the river of the sky. Ishaan felt like a castaway. If only he could bottle a message in his vapour and fling it at the sky, someone might just find it and come to his rescue, come to their rescue. O Kalidas! Thou shouldst be living at this hour.

Ishaan looked at the mountains in front of him. Jagged leviathans of oceanic rock tossed up towards heaven when the subcontinent collided with Asia, many, many eons ago. They had aged. The heavy snow on their heads coloured them with the colour of maturity. What wisdom could they have accumulated down the ages! No one to tell about it, except for the clouds. Ishaan breathed. The clouds emptied themselves into the rivers and the rivers carried all this wisdom off into the very depths of the ocean. Deep, deep inside, where Vishnu slept on his *Ananata*, and Laxmi sat at his feet. Maybe he knew. Maybe he could tell Ishaan what these mountains in front of him were thinking all the time. Ishaan shrugged his shoulder. Fantasy, fairytales that Ma used to tell him. Bedtime stories. Yes, that's what these Puranic tales were. Bedtime stories. Gods, demons, Avatars. Stupid, silly bedtime stories. His caste, the Brahmins had used this fantastic nonsense to lull the nation to sleep for ages, while the rest of the world marched ahead down the path of progress. How else could a band of firangi bandits from a tiny island in the North Atlantic Ocean have stomped on our heads for two hundred years? While we fought over what to eat and what not to eat, whom to touch and whom not to touch, these fucking firangis lorded over us, treating us like dogs! It is better, far better to be a staunch atheist than a superstitious fool. Ishaan felt relieved that he had discarded his *janeu* a long time back. He was no longer carrying that mark of disgrace. But was this the time to wonder about firangis and brahmins? He was a fucking plane crash survivor! He should be thinking of somehow returning to safety and civilization. Maybe the ATC back in Kathmandu was aware of this incident. They must be! How far was he from Kathmandu? Two hundred, three hundred kilometers tops. They must be scrambling rescue parties right now. The radar blip had suddenly disappeared on their screen. They must be in the know! It was only a matter of time before helicopters would start whizzing around them, filling the mountain air with their comforting droning noise. Ishaan could literally hear the helicopters at this point. Or he thought he did. Chop, chop, chop … ah, the sound of civilization!

"Hey, mate! Come inside, quick!" Richard yelled from inside the cabin. Ishaan was suddenly jolted away from his pacifying daydream back to the real world. "What is it?" he yelled back while running into the cabin. Richard was carrying a girl by the shoulders, helping her to her feet. It was the Nepali girl with the purse and black sneakers. Ishaan shrieked in amazement. "She's alive, mate! She's alive!" Richard exclaimed.

Ishaan quickly ran up to her assistance. Together the two men helped the girl to a comfortable sitting position on the floor. Ishaan quickly checked her for cuts and bruises. There was a deep gash on her forehead. Blood was oozing out of it and covering her left eye. Ishaan quickly tore off some gauze and wiped the blood clean with some alcohol. The girl made a slight exclamation of pain and discomfort. But she wasn't completely conscious at that point. She was in a daze. The concussion on her head was zipping her back and forth between light and darkness. Ishaan knew exactly how she felt. He himself had felt that a little while ago when he had woken up in his bed of snow. "We need to let her rest, Richard. Maybe pour a little vodka down her throat … that'll warm her up." Ishaan looked up at Richard.

"Here ya go, mate," Richard said while handing him the bottle of White Mischief.

Ishaan gently opened the girl's lips with his fingers and slid in the opening of the bottle. He gently tilted the bottle and saw with satisfaction as the liquid glided down into her mouth. He then gently held her by her chin and tilted her head upwards. The vodka made a gulping sound in her throat. He then took the bottle away from her mouth and stood up. "Want a drink?" he asked Richard.

"Sure, mate! Or else the cold might freeze our balls!"

Ishaan laughed. For the first time, in a long time, he laughed. The plane crash didn't matter. The deaths didn't matter. The future didn't matter. All that now mattered was the bottle of vodka in his hand and the smiling face of Richard in front of his eyes. They had survived! That was reason enough to celebrate.

Ishaan took a sip of the vodka and handed over the bottle to Richard. The liquor was strong. He gulped it down with a contorted face. He looked at Richard. He took two shots and looked at Ishaan with squinted eyes, his face equally contorted. "That's some strong stuff …" he said to Ishaan after gulping down the vodka.

"By the way, where did you find it, buddy?" asked Ishaan.

"Over there …" Richard said while pointing to a broken trolly way up the aisle. "There are a couple more of these over there."

"That's good … we'll need that to keep ourselves sane up here," Ishaan answered with some satisfaction, "Besides, alcohol is a miracle liquid. You can drink it; you can use it to disinfect wounds and you can also use it to preserve things."

"You'll know better, doc," answered Richard with a wry smile on his lips.

Ishaan looked up at Richard. He was tall, probably six feet two inches, with a broad chest and strong arms. His hair was the colour of straw and so were his thin eyebrows. He was clean-shaved, with a chiselled chin and pink lips. His eyes were brown. They may have looked bright under normal circumstances. But the present situation had taken a heavy toll on their brightness. They looked dull and weary. Full of care. "I'm sorry for the loss of your baby," Ishaan finally blurted out after some hesitation.

"It's not your fault, mate …You did the best you could to save my wife's life …" Richard answered, looking straight into his eyes. There was gratitude in his gaze. "Here ya go, mate," Richard said while handing the bottle over to Ishaan.

Ishaan took one drink and looked up at the horizon. The Sun was already on its downward trajectory. What was the time? He looked at his watch. 3:18 pm. "Do you think they'll come looking for us?" he asked Richard.

Richard cupped his hands together and blew into them and answered, "That's what I'm betting my life on. If the cold doesn't kill us, the darkness will."

"I didn't quite get you …" said Ishaan, puzzled.

"Ya see, mate, these mountains up here are the habitat of Himalayan Snow Leopards," Richard said while pointing to the mountains in front of them. "We've crashed smack in the middle of their territory. They are not generally aggressive towards humans, but who knows. They're wild beasts for Chrissake!"

"How do you know all that?" asked Ishaan, both impressed and alarmed.

"I work with National Geographic," Richard answered calmly, his eyes fixed on the mountains.

"Ah ... ah ..." the noise was coming from inside the cabin.

The two men turned around. The Nepali girl was regaining consciousness. It was she who was making the noise. They quickly rushed to her side. Ishaan sat on the floor with her while Richard bent down, his hands on his knees.

"Whe … where am I?" she asked, still in a daze.

Ishaan held her by her shoulder and calmly said, "Listen to me … do not panic … listen carefully …"

The girl turned to him, her eyes searching Ishaan's face for answers.

"You were in a plane … do you remember?"

The girl nodded in agreement, "Yes. I was on my way to Delhi…" she said, still puzzled.

"Yes, that plane has crashed …"

The girl shrieked, "What!"

"Shhh …" Ishaan put a finger on her lips, "… there's a critically wounded woman over there …" he said while pointing at Richard's wife, who was still lying unconscious.

The girl followed his fingers and saw her. She then muffled her mouth with her hands and looked wildly around. Richard was staring at her.

"O my God … o my God …" the girl said, "I need to call Papa …"

"You can't …" Ishaan told her, looking straight into her eyes.

"Why?"

"We are way up in the mountains … there's no network here."

The girl sprang to her feet.

"Hey, easy, lady," Richard said, holding her hand, "No need to rush. There's only death all around."

The two men helped the girl to the open end of the cabin. The girl looked at the snowy mountains with sheer dread in her eyes. Ishaan held her hand and said, "Don't panic …"

The girl quickly tore her hand away from his and exclaimed, "Don't touch me. I'm fine."

"Hey … we just saved your life. Have a bit of gratitude, lady," Richard hit back at her.

The girl looked at the two men, her head bobbing from one to the other. The only other living individual was a critically wounded woman. All of a sudden she felt like a prisoner. She was at the mercy of these two unknown men, way up in the Himalayan mountains. These two could do anything with her and no one would ever know. It filled her with sheer dread. She started breathing heavily, slowly inching away from them, backwards. Her face was becoming red.

Ishaan said, "Hey … hey … relax. They will be coming for us soon. Don't panic. And we won't do anything to you. This guy over here," he said pointing to Richard, " … is married. The injured woman is his wife. And I … I have a girlfriend back in Delhi," Ishaan lied.

"That's no reason for you to not rape me," the girl said while eying Ishaan suspiciously.

Richard guffawed, "O come on … are you serious, lady? Rape you? Here?" he paused for an answer, "We guys are scared shitless and you should be too. We are all waiting for the search party to arrive … my wife is seriously hurt. And this gentleman over here is a doctor," he said while pointing to Ishaan. "He pulled out a metal shard from my wife's abdomen and he revived you. You should be thanking him and not calling him a potential rapist … for Chrissake!" Richard was angry; his face red as a tomato.

The girl's gaze softened. She looked first at Richard and then at Ishaan. And then she burst out crying.

"Ri … Richard …" a female voice came from inside the cabin, weak with exhaustion. It was Richard's wife. She had gained consciousness. Richard sprang to his feet and ran to her side. Ishaan and the girl followed just behind him.

"I'm here, lovey, I'm right here," Richard whispered to her.

Ishaan was standing next to Richard while the girl was standing behind them, peeking between the two men for a sight of her.

The woman looked at all three of them, and then looked at her belly. It was girdled with a scarf soaked in vodka, with dried blood tinging its edges. She screamed, "My baby!" and then she burst out crying, "My baby … my baby … O ah ahhh," she was shrieking and sobbing helplessly.

Richard held her face in his palms and said, his voice choked with emotions, "Shhh, darling, you get well first. Our baby didn't want to come to us right away, ya, see … so he slipped right back to heaven. He'll come to us when we are ready," he then kissed her forehead.

The woman grabbed his hands in both her palms and cried piteously.

Ishaan couldn't hold back his tears. He turned away and silently wept. The girl came up behind him and held his shoulder. Ishaan turned. She too was weeping.

The sun had slid under the horizon and darkness had started enveloping the snow. Its dying light had tinged the mountains crimson, with a dash of yellow at the top. The three were sitting at the entrance to the cabin. Riley, Richard's wife, was sleeping on the floor. They had prepared for her a bed with whatever materials they could salvage. Cloth, coverings of the seats, sweaters, jackets. Whatever they could get their hands on, they used it to make a bed as soft as they could for her. She had three jackets covering her body. They themselves were dressed for the terrible cold. Ishaan wore three sweaters under his jacket. The girl who had introduced herself as Uma wore two jackets atop her clothes, and five woolen scarfs, two her own and three salvaged. Richard wore only one jacket. He had given the other two to Riley. They had cleared the cabin of dead bodies. There had been five dead bodies inside it. Ishaan felt terrible pain while giving the little Punjabi girl her premature burial under the snow. He had wept bitterly. Her father was not found. Now, to get over the strain of the work and lighten themselves up, the three were drinking vodka and talking their worries off.

Ishaan watched as the last traces of the day evaporated from the tops of the snowy peaks, leaving only darkness behind. The two share the World between them, the Light and the Dark, each ruling it for half the day. Or maybe they are like two star-crossed lovers who chase each other endlessly, never meeting, never consummating their love. Like Radha and Krishna. The eternal unconsummated love affair. Ishaan sighed. He looked at Richard. He was gathering cushions torn from the seats, pieces of cloth—anything that could be burnt, and heaping all of that together in front of the cabin. He planned to light a bonfire. A fresh bottle of White Mischief stood on the snow near him. The fire would serve two purposes. Firstly, it'll keep them warm, keep them alive. And, secondly, what Richard and Ishaan were more concerned about, was that it will keep away any predators. Snow Leopards, in this case. They hadn't told anything about the leopards to Uma. She might just start panicking all over again. The crash, the cold and the deaths were enough already for all three of them. Now there was the added threat of big cats. It was better to keep Uma in the dark about it, the two had agreed. Ishaan looked at Uma. She was fiddling with a Rudraksha bead; her eyes closed in prayer. Ishaan felt like laughing. Seriously! After all of this, she still believed in God? In miracles? Ishaan stood up. He headed down to where Richard was and stood by his side. Richard looked up at him, kneeling over the inflammables, his hands busy with the work. "Need help, buddy?" he asked Richard.

"Na … just stay alive. That'll be help enough …" Richard answered, his eyes locked into Ishaan's.

Ishaan knelt down. "What do you do exactly in National Geography?"

"I'm a photographer, mate. Wildlife photography … that's my bread and butter …" Richard poured some vodka on the heap and started searching his pockets for a light.

"Here," Ishaan quickly took out his Zippo and gave it to Richard.

"Ya sure are handy, mate," Richard answered him with a smile, taking the lighter from his hand. He lit the fire in a jiffy. The blaze cast long shadows of the two on the walls of the cabin. The shadow of Uma was seen sitting, her legs huddled together in sitting position. She was still praying.

The two men looked at each other. "Do you think they'll really come looking for us?" Ishaan asked Richard.

"That's protocol, mate, but, fuck protocol … that's sheer humanity. They mustn't be dumb fucks to not know that one of their flights has crashed and that there just might be survivors who were freezing their asses off in the terrible cold of the upper Himalayas …"

"Can you guess how high up we really are?" Ishaan asked while fiddling with his watch. There was no altimeter in it. There should have been one.

Richard looked around a bit and said, "I'm guessing we're three thousand or three and a half thousand meters above sea level … but that's just a guess."

Ishaan sighed, "Bloody hell!"

"That's just the beginning of the problem, mate," Richard went on, "it's a miracle that not one of us has had altitude sickness up until now. These mountains have a way of getting into people's heads, playing with their minds … it'll start with breathlessness. The oxygen supply to the brain gets reduced at these heights. You'll start feeling dizzy … then your thoughts will start getting distorted … you'll not be able to think clearly …" Richard said while putting his finger to his head, "Then comes the interesting part. The distinction between Reality and Fantasy will be slowly erased …" Richard stopped and looked at Uma. He pointed at her and said, "Look at her. She's praying. She's praying to someone … probably one of the many gods that Hindus have … if she gets altitude sickness, she just might get a vision of that god …"

Ishaan got the cue. He smiled at Richard and said, "Yup … that's what visions are all about … when air travels downwards, it's called fart … when it travels upwards, it's called spirituality."

Richard burst out laughing. "That's the point, mate," he said between laughs.

"And that's the case with all visions of angels or gods or demons … fart going to your brain," Ishaan added with extra satisfaction.

The two were literally baiting Uma. She knew it. She slowly opened her eyes, looking straight at Ishaan she said, "You two can laugh all you want … but I have my reasons for believing."

"Believing in what?" Ishaan asked.

Uma paused, took a deep breath, looked up at the mountains and pointed to them. Then she said slowly, "I believe in the Man in these mountains … he'll save me."

The two men looked at the mountains. Then they turned towards her. "Who?" asked Richard, his eyes playing with her features, waiting for her to giggle, waiting for her to snap out of her infantile fantasies.

Ishaan understood whom she was referring to.

"Who is it, lady?" Richard asked again, "There's not another goddamn human for hundreds of miles around … no one to save you, but yourself."

Uma didn't answer him but stood staring sternly at the mountains, as they glistened into view under the moonlight.

"She's talking of Siva …" Ishaan answered for her, dragging his eyes away from Uma towards Richard.

Richard was scandalized. "Bullshit!" he exclaimed and picked up the bottle of vodka from the snow and took a sip.

Ishaan looked at Uma. Her eyes still had that fixed gaze in them, unmoving, unruffled. She was fixed in her conviction. He took the bottle from Richard and took a sip. Then he turned towards Uma again and said, "Come here, near the fire. Siva is not going to use his third eye from the mountains to warm you up ... and bring some cloth to sit on." He spread a piece of cloth on the snow and sat down. Richard followed suit. But Uma just stood there, staring at the glistening mountains. The moonlight had painted them a brilliant white. It was soothing to look at, like Ma's soft touch. And not like the dazzling brilliance of the daytime that hurt the eyes. Ishaan looked up at the night sky. Stars gleamed there, millions and millions of stars, millions and millions of lightyears away. There was no light pollution up here, at this height. The night sky was visible in brilliant, vivid detail. Ishaan could make out the faint outlines of the Milky Way, or the Akash Ganga. Our galaxy. Earth is just a tiny tiny speck of dust orbiting a flint of light that we call the sun, which itself is just a small, nearly insignificant pearl strewn into the necklace called the Milky Way. And there were billions upon billions of other such necklaces which were there in the jewel box of the heavens. It was as if Mother Nature had flung open her jewel box for Ishaan to peek into. Such beauty, such ruthlessness! Mother Nature is an enigma. One moment the caring, doting Mother ... the next moment Rana Chandi, ruthless, her lolling tongue dripping fresh blood ... Ishaan remembered a Bengali devotional song that Ma used to sing during her puja ... it went something like ...

Shyama Kokhono Purush, Kokhono Prakriti
Kokhono Shunyakara He ...

Mayer Se Bhabo Bhabia Komolakanta
Sohoje Pagol Holo Re …
Shyama Ma ki Amar Kalo?

Shyama is Purusha at times, at times Prakriti, and at times Nothingness … thinking of this Kamalakanta easily loses his mind … Is Shyama Ma of mine Black?

He looked at Uma. She was staring blankly at the moon, her hand fiddling with the Rudraksha bead around her neck. The moon was a glimmering crescent on the horizon. Maybe, it was the waxing phase or the waning phase, Ishaan couldn't tell. "Come now … sit here. It's warm around the fire. You might just die of hypothermia … you can't cheat death twice, you know," he said while patting the snow next to him.

Uma looked at him, "Yeah, I'm coming." She then went inside and came out with a cloth. She spread it next to the fire and sat down.

"Here, help yourself," Richard said, offering her the bottle of vodka.

She took it, put the bottle to her mouth and gulped down some of it. Her face immediately contorted. She took out the bottle from her mouth and immediately gave it back to Richard. Then she stuck out her tongue right down to her chin and exclaimed, "Ah … ugh … how do you guys drink this!" while rubbing her lips with the back of her palm.

Richard burst out laughing. He laughed for a while and then said, "This thing brought you back to consciousness, lady. Give it some respect." He then drank some vodka and gave the bottle over to Ishaan.

Ishaan took the bottle in his hands and looked at Uma, a wry smile playing on his lips, "Have you never drunk vodka?"

"Duh ... I study at JNU back in Delhi. I've done things you guys couldn't imagine. But I've never drunk neat vodka," Uma replied, a tinge of pride passing over her face.

"Really?" Ishaan pretended to look surprised. "Please, regale us with your adventures as a psychonaut," he added.

Uma paused for a while. She looked at Richard. He was all ears too. "Well ... I've done weed, N10, gin ..."

"Hey ... gin is a tonic ..." Richard cut her off.

"Let me continue ..." she went on, "... I'm not finished."

"Carry on ..." Ishaan said.

"Yeah ... gin, tornado ..."

"What's tornado?" Richard asked her.

Ishaan answered on her behalf, "It's when you smoke weed and cigarettes together ... it's called tornado."

"Oh!"

"Then I've done den ..."

"What's den?" Richard interrupted again.

"Dendrite ..." Ishaan replied.

"Hey, I'm not gonna say anything if you keep jutting in like that ..." Uma rebuked Richard. Her anger was cute.

"Okay, okay ... my bad," Richard said while putting his hands up in the air.

"That's about it," she said after some hesitation and fell silent, staring at the fire and putting her palms out to greet the heat.

Ishaan looked at Uma and said, "Listen."

She looked at him. He looked straight into her eyes and said, "You've not done half the things that you said you did. You're only saying all that to look cool ..."

"How ... why ... why would I try to look cool?"

"Cause, if you really had done all those things, they would have taken a heavy toll on your body. You look fresh enough. You probably have done weed with cigarettes, that's all."

"How do you know?"

"Cause, I've done all those and way way more … I know what happens to the body when you stay high on those things. Besides, I'm a doctor … I can read the body of my patients with my bare eyes."

Richard was pretending to look away; his lips curled in a smile. Uma had locked her eyes with Ishaan's. It was the matter of her prestige. "No … no … I'm telling the truth," she looked at Richard.

Richard caught her gaze and burst out laughing. "Ho, ho … see, lady, where I come from, we have weed for breakfast, LSD for lunch and Meth for dinner … you can't cheat me."

Uma's face shrivelled up with humiliation. She fixed her gaze on the fire, without even blinking. "It's okay …" Ishaan whispered to her after a while, "… you're young. We also did such things when we were your age … we also wanted to look cool," he added for emphasis.

Uma slowly looked up at him, her eyes brimming with tears of humiliation. They were literally asking for clemency. Ishaan patted her back, "So tell me … what do you study at JNU?"

"Hi … History," she answered slowly.

"Which year?"

"BA second year."

"That's good."

"Indian History or Nepali History?" Richard asked, puzzled.

"It's something we both share. India and Nepal have this roti-beti system … which means interdining and intermarriage. We're not that different you know," Ishaan explained.

"But China sure is poking its long red nose into your roti-beti now, isn't it, mate?" Richard put in while poking the fire with his boot.

"Yeah … that's not entirely incorrect …" said Ishaan hesitantly, feeling a tad uncomfortable.

Uma blurted out, "Nepal is a free country. It's free to decide whom to have relations with and what those relations should be. No other country has the right to dictate to it what to do and what not to do," while staring straight at the fire.

Ishaan was looking at the fire too. Suddenly things were getting uncomfortable. "See," he said slowly after some time, "… the way I see it, it is slave mentality. We guys in this corner of the earth have spent so much time under the boots of the Brits that we have lost the ability to see each other's progress without boiling over with jealousy. Nepal, Bangladesh, Sri Lanka … I'm not even mentioning Pakistan … are all jealous of India's progress. Sure, India too is not without its faults. It has committed countless blunders with respect to its relations with these countries. The LTTE in Sri Lanka has had the silent sympathy of all the Tamils and the behaviour of Indian media personnel during the Kathmandu earthquake surely isn't praiseworthy … but … that's because of the slave mentality. It works both ways. The Brits looked upon us as slaves, and when they went, we started looking at each other as slaves. It's just like a pot of live crabs … whenever one crab tries to crawl up, the others hold it down with all their might … but things will change," Ishaan looked up at Richard, "India accounted for twenty five percent of global GDP before the Brits landed here, and mark my words, before this century is over, India shall again account for the lion's share of the global GDP …" his face started to redden and his eyes glowed with an unnatural fervour, "The Brits looted India of all its wealth … it was the pagoda tree. You just shake it and money would fall down … they looted the Kohinoor … they broke the looms of Bengal weavers and smashed their thumbs … they systematically deindustrialized the land so that Manchester cloth could flood Indian markets … we literally paid for our own slavery. They took all our wealth away and financed their Industrial Revolution … they fattened on our blood, those bloody vampires!" Ishaan spat on the snow, his eyes burning hot, "And they got what they deserved … the two World Wars came as retribution. Imperial Britain met its doppelganger in Nazi Germany and soon came to naught. That's Karma … whatever you do comes back to you with compound interest. It's only a matter of time before India regains its lost prestige as the Queen of the World and Britain is relegated to its puny place on the shores of Europe again …" his voice almost a thundering roar at this point. The two men looked each other in the eye.

Uma's head was bobbing from one man to the other. The air was tense, when suddenly Riley, Richard's wife, called from the inside.

"Richard … Richard …"

Richard sprang to his feet and ran inside saying, "I'm right here, lovey … I'm right here."

Ishaan and Uma sat looking at the fire. Neither said anything. After some time Richard came back. He patted Ishaan on the back and said, "I understand your righteous indignation, mate, but my wife needs to sleep … you're a doctor after all."

Ishaan apologized, "I'm sorry, man, it's just that I get very excited while talking about these things … I'm sorry … I really am."

No one talked much after that. They all silently sat there, drinking vodka and passing the bottle to each other.

Ishaan looked up at the starlit sky. The Milky Way, Galaxy, or the *Akash Ganga* was clearly visible from this altitude. He stared hard into the depths of the Universe and the Universe stared back at him, blinking through a myriad of stars and galaxies. Nature always reciprocates our actions, Ishaan thought. Whether there is a God or not is not the issue; the important thing is that there is Karma. It's nature's way of talking back to you, to make you account for the wrongs you have done and to reward you for what you did right. Every action one takes is destined to leave consequences behind. There is no escaping from the consequences of our actions. If he is miserable now, it must be because of some past actions, actions he committed knowingly or unknowingly. Was he not aware that the wanton lifestyle he led was causing injury to his body, scars which might emerge later in the form of cancer or liver sclerosis? But one thing was certain, there was no need for a God in a world governed by Karma.

Uma suddenly got up and said, "Let me go and check if there's something to eat on the plane. We haven't eaten anything the whole day."

"Try your luck. I searched the cabin through and through and all I could find were these," Richard replied while holding up three bottles of vodka, glistening in the light of the campfire.

Uma didn't answer him and headed straight for the cabin, while the light from her flashlight led the way.

Richard looked at Ishaan and said, "Never breathe a word to her about the leopards; she'll go bonkers over it." Ishaan replied with a nod. After a pause, Richard said, "I wonder what leopard meat would taste like," with a faint smile playing on his lips.

"We don't have to eat each other, do we?" Ishaan replied with a faint smile playing on his lips. "Don't know, mate," Richard's face lit up, "… if the rescuers don't show up in time, the survivors might just have to resort to good old cannibalism."

"No one has to eat each other." The two suddenly were startled by Uma's voice. Uma was coming towards them with something wrapped in aluminium foils. The foil reflected the campfire and looked like gold. Uma came up to them and said, "See, I've found some food. We only need to warm it up and eat." The three quickly tore open the foil and found a couple of burgers and sandwiches.

Richard quickly took out a sandwich and held it to the fire from a reasonable distance. "This one's for my wife," he said while warming the sandwich.

Richard left the two beside the fire and headed straight for the cabin with the sandwich. Riley needed to eat badly, especially since she had lost a large amount of blood.

Ishaan looked at Uma and said, "Where did you find it … this food?"

Uma said flippantly, "Let's just say that I got lucky … here, have a burger."

Ishaan took the burger from Uma's hand and held it towards the fire. The cheese in the burger was nearly frozen due to the cold. Ishaan remembered the blonde woman at the airport cafeteria who had been eating a burger and feeding her child pieces of it. Richard came back in some time, and the three silently ate whatever was left inside the foil with immense satisfaction.

After some time Richard looked at his watch, "It's seven thirty, mate. We should catch some zees. You guys head inside. I'll put some more fuel into the fire … make sure it keeps on burning … I'll sleep later." He then winked at Ishaan.

Ishaan got the cue. It was about the leopards. He said, "All right ... we'll head inside. Come, Uma," he said while tugging at her arm.

They clambered onto the cabin. They both were very, very drunk. The vodka and the Himalayan cold had worked in tandem to drum up the symphony of deep inebriation. They were high, both literally and figuratively. Uma carelessly settled down on a seat near the cockpit, while Ishaan found his near a window. He laid down. These seats felt like cushions of silk to him. All that now mattered was sleep. He wasn't hungry. He wasn't thirsty. He was just sleepy ... very, very sleepy. He drifted off...

"Will you marry me?" It was *her*. She was looking at him. They were lying together naked in bed in his flat in Delhi. They had just made love. *Her* plump breasts were resting on his chest. His arms were around her body. *Her* brown hair was all in a mess. Ishaan took a lock of her hair and wound it around the top of her head, backwards. He then kissed *her* lips. "Will you marry me, Ishaan?" *she* asked again.

"That's the silliest question I've ever heard," Ishaan said to her.

"*Matlab?*" *she* was beginning to sit up, *her* eyes beginning to tinge with indignation and scorn. "Shh ... shhh ..." Ishaan put his finger on *her* lips. He held *her* tighter, "You just asked a man lost in the desert, dying of thirst, whether he'd like to drink zam zam."

Her face lit up immediately. *She* fell over him, kissing his face, "My *Shona* Goblu ..."

"Stop calling me that!" Ishaan snapped.

She burst out laughing, "You bongs are so cute ... you have such cute pet names, Goblu," *she* kissed him again. "I'm gonna name our first child Goblu. Goblu Mirza Chakravorty," *she* said, fingering his right nipple.

"Why have surnames in the first place?" Ishaan retorted, "Surnames divide people. If you really want to name our first child Goblu, then just name him Goblu. Simply Goblu. Period."

She looked into his eyes and said, "You take this communal divide business seriously, Ishaan. Come on. It's just a cultural thing. I have Irani blood in me, so I feel proud of my surname. Our child will inherit my blood. I want to give him the pride that I myself feel. And 'Chakravorty'… it's more like 'Chakravartin'… like great Indian Emperors of the past had … like Chakravartin Samrat Ashok. Our child will inherit both our surnames. Come on, don't be a spoilt sport." Ishaan laid *her* down beside him, "You can name our child whatever you want, but for that to happen we must first get married. Will your parents permit?"

Her forehead immediately wrinkled. *She* lowered her gaze to his chest. Then after a moment *she* looked up at him and said, "It's not Ammu that I'm worried about … it's Abbu …"

"Come on … you guys are Shia … you can't be that *kattar*. Hindus and Shias understand each other well."

Her face lit up with a smile, "Idea! We'll run away," *she* said while snapping her fingers in excitement. "When we have our first child, then we'll come back and ask for forgiveness. Abbu's heart will melt when he will look at the face of his grandchild. After all, I'm his only child. He can't be mad at us forever," *she* went on weaving her plans in the air. Ishaan simply looked at *her* face. He couldn't hear a word that *she* was saying. All his attention was fixed on *her* bright, beautiful face. That smile. Those eyes. Those lips. Those locks of hair. Ah … if there is paradise on earth, it is this, it is this, it is this. *Gar firdaus bar-rue zamin ast, hami asto, hamin asto, hamin ast.*

"Wake up … wake up!" Uma yelled at the top of her voice.

Ishaan sat up with a start. He looked at her puzzled, "What happened?"

"Riley's missing," Uma answered.

"What do you mean she's missing … she can't go anywhere. She's seriously wounded …"

"I don't know where she went. Richard has gone out looking for her. You need to come, quick."

Together the two scrambled out of the cabin. There were faint traces of blood on the snow … they followed the blood trail. Just a few steps into their journey, they heard it. "Oh God! Oh fucking God! Ahhh …," It was Richard's voice. He was kneeling over something on the snow, clutching it with all his might and crying the most heart-rending cry that Ishaan had ever heard. There was horror, anguish and rage in it. They ran towards him. The snow sank beneath their feet, yet they still ran. They got the picture when they had come within a yard of Richard. Riley's body lay there. Torn up to shreds. The snow around her body was pink with blood. Her bones were sticking out from the crevices of her corpse. Richard was hugging this half-eaten corpse to his bosom and crying his heart out.

VISHUDDHA

The horror! Oh, the horror! Ishaan's head was reeling. He slumped backwards. His stomach began turning. He turned around and puked. Only slime came out. There was nothing else to throw up. The slime fell on the snow and glistened like dew in the light of the morning sun. He wiped his lips with the back of his palm and looked at Uma. She was kneeling on the snow, her fists clenched, her face contorted. She made a noise, "Ugh … ugh …" She was gonna pop. And pop she did. The snow in front of her soon began glistening with her slime. Ishaan looked at Richard. He was unresponsive. Froth hung from his lips. His eyes were bloodshot and wide open. He just clung onto his wife's body with all his might, looking straight at her face and almost whispering from time to time, "Oh God … oh God …" Her cheeks were missing. So were her eyes. They had been gobbled up. Her throat had a deep gash in it. Her windpipe had been torn off. The cross around her neck dangled down to the right, almost touching the pink snow beneath, but missed it by a hair's breadth.

It reminded Ishaan of Michelangelo's 'Creation of Adam'. God was just a hair's breadth away from man. And he always will be. Richard needed his assistance. He bent down to where Richard was kneeling and held his shoulders with both his hands. Richard didn't even feel his touch.

Ishaan shook his shoulder, "Richard ... buddy ... get a hold of yourself."

Richard didn't even hear him. He kept on whispering, "Oh God ... oh God ..."

Ishaan shook him again, this time more vehemently.

Richard cast a wild glance at Ishaan, his eyes beaming insanity. "Get off me ... get your bloody hands off me!" he yelled at Ishaan.

"Richard ... Richard, come to your senses. She's dead ..." Ishaan said, readying himself for a wrestling bout with this man crazed by his loss.

"She's not dead ... just sleeping ... can't you see!" Richard's eyes had an unnatural vigour in them.

Ishaan quickly snapped at Uma. She was watching the two of them like a kitten. Ishaan winked at her, pointing at Riley's body. She got the cue. Ishaan would lure away Richard and Uma had to move Riley's body in the meantime. That was the only way to bring Richard to his senses. "Sure, mate, let her sleep ... we need to bring her things from the plane, or else she's gonna catch a cold. Let's go," Ishaan said to Richard, trying to sound as natural as possible, keeping his eyes fixed on Richard's eyes.

"I ain't goin' anywhere. I'll stay right here with her," Richard answered, his voice sounding as if coming from far off.

Ishaan realized that he had no choice. He had to wrestle Richard away from the corpse. He quickly bent forward and grabbed Richard from the back and pulled with all his strength. Richard hit back at him with a punch. The punch landed on his belly, but the impact was cushioned by the multiple sweaters he wore. Ishaan used his forearm and biceps to hook onto his neck from behind. He had to strangle Richard. He dragged Richard away from the corpse towards the plane. Richard was kicking and yelling continuously. Finally, Richard put his hands backwards and grabbed a fistful of Ishaan's hair. His hair was long. It hurt a lot. Still, Ishaan didn't give up. He kept on strangling Richard and dragging him away from the corpse. But then Richard threw a back punch. His fist crashed on Ishaan's chin.

"Ahhh!" Ishaan yelled out and let go of his hold. Richard immediately sprang to his feet and leapt at Ishaan. The two men wrestled in the snow. Ishaan was five ten and Richard was six two. It was a close fight. But both were very weak due to exhaustion. The two rolled on the snow. Once it was Ishaan, who had the upper hand and landed punches against his opponent. Again, it was the other way around. This lasted for a while, when finally Richard leapt onto Ishaan's chest and pinned him to the ground with his right hand. His left hand deftly landed three successive punches at Ishaan's face. Ishaan ducked two of them, but the third landed on his nose. "Oh Ma!" Ishaan let out a shrill cry. His nose immediately started bleeding. Then suddenly Uma came up from behind and hit Richard with something. Thud. Richard limped over Ishaan's body, unconscious. Ishaan laid Richard down on the snow beside him and stood up while covering his nose with his right hand. He looked at Uma. There was a broken steel rod in her hands.

Ishaan looked at Uma's face. It was red with excitement, anger and shock. She let the rod fall to the ground and reeled backwards, her hands on her head. "Oh my God!" she exclaimed out loud.

Ishaan rubbed off the blood sprouting from his nose with the back of his palms and said, "Are you okay?" while putting his hand on her back.

"I'm fine. I'm fine ..." she answered in between deep breaths. The two looked at Richard. He lay unconscious on the snow. Ishaan quickly went to him and turned him over.

He checked for his breath. Yes, he was breathing. He checked his pulse. It was beating slowly. He then got up and said to Uma, "We've got to tie him up."

She assented with a nod. Together, the two dragged Richard to the cabin and tied up his hands tightly against a seat. They also tied up his legs. Richard lay there, his head drooping down on his chest. Ishaan sat near him. Uma kept standing. They looked at each other for a while. Then she turned in the direction of Riley's body and exclaimed, "Who or what could have done that to her? My God!"

Ishaan didn't answer her. He kept looking down at the floor; his gaze fixed on a crack in its metal panelling. How could he now tell her of the leopards? It was too late already. Richard had been right. The leopards didn't attack any of them but took the easiest prey. The ailing Riley. She couldn't fight back. The poor woman was probably asleep when the leopard came and attacked her, dragging her by the throat. But how could that have happened if Richard had been awake? He certainly would have scared it away or called them for help. He too must have fallen asleep, heavily sedated with the booze … the attack must have happened around dawn. The fire must have gone out without Richard tending it. It all made sense now. Ishaan looked up at Uma and said, "I think we better bury Riley's body before Richard wakes up? Don't you think?" he pondered as he looked into her eyes. Uma took a look at Richard's unconscious body and looked back at Ishaan. "The only way to make Richard come to his senses is to dispose of her body fast … that corpse is pegging him down to insanity," he added with emphasis.

Uma nodded her approval and said, "Yes … you're right. This is probably gonna be the sorriest day of my life, burying a woman's body while her husband lay unconscious and tied up." She wiped her nose with her sleeve.

Together the two dug a grave for Riley in the snow. While burying her body, Ishaan took off the cross from her neck, or whatever was left of it. He looked at Uma and said, "Should we keep it or bury it?"

"Why do you want to keep it?"

"If any of us makes it back, we can give this cross to her closest living relative as a memento … but it'll remind Richard of her … so we shouldn't give it to him. What do you think?"

Uma wondered for a while. Then she put out her hand and said, "Okay, give it to me. I'll keep it safe."

Ishaan gave the cross to her. She put it around her neck, along with the Rudraksha beads, and covered it up with her jacket and scarves. The two started walking back towards the plane, kicking the snow on the way. "I still don't understand. What could have done that to her …?" Uma wondered aloud.

"It was a leopard. A Himalayan snow leopard," Ishaan blurted out, unable to contain himself anymore.

Uma stopped in her tracks, "What! How do you know that?"

"Richard told me about them … yesterday. You were unconscious," Ishaan said while trying to look at Uma, but he failed miserably. "He told me that these mountains are the habitat of these leopards … they generally don't attack humans but … as you can see …" he said while pointing at Riley's grave.

Uma looked dumbfounded. Then she yelled, "Oh, you stupid bastards!" Her face was red with anger. Ishaan looked at her, puzzled. "Oh, you stupid fucking bastards! You simply could have told me that," she said while bending down over the snow. She hid her face in her palms. She was weeping.

Ishaan was confused. "What is it? How would have that helped? Having told you about the leopards?"

She didn't answer. She just wept. After a while she stood up, wiping her face with her palms and sleeves. Then she did something which amazed and frightened Ishaan. She took out a kukri from her jacket. Holding it up at his face she finally said, "I've been hiding this under my clothes since yesterday … I found it in the wreckage … I was keeping it with me in case anyone of you men turned on me. You could have simply told me about the leopards. I would have gladly given it to you."

Ishaan moved his eyes from the kukri to Uma and back again. Then he finally said, "Keep it, might come in handy later. We were worried that the news of the leopards might frighten you, so we hid it from you."

"But you could have saved her life if you hadn't hidden it from me."

Ishaan didn't answer. There was no answer to this. He simply walked towards the plane, his head hanging down in shame and remorse.

The two came and sat near Richard. The poor man was still unconscious. Neither said anything. They simply sat there, staring at the snow. Could this get any worse? Ishaan wondered. *Jole kumir, dangay bagh.* Crocodile in the water, tiger on the land. If they didn't die of the cold, they would certainly die of the leopards. The only option left was to fight back. Fight the cold and fight the cats. Ishaan remembered something. A fragment of a poem he had read in school … the poet … yes, the poet was P. B. Shelley …

> *I silently laugh at my own cenotaph*
> *And out of the caverns of rain. Like a*
> *Child from the womb, like a ghost from*
> *The tomb, I arise and unbuild it again …*

Death is certain. It is inevitable. But that is no reason to not fight back, not delay it. The sign of Life is Motion, Resistance. Inertia is Death. Stopping means dying. The world can throw anything at you, but you must be man enough to shoulder the burden … to move on despite all obstacles … if he could make it this far, he could go further. Ma used to say something— a quotation, *'Strength is Life, Weakness is Death.'* Vivekananda. She admired Vivekananda. Ishaan was not into Vivekananda, but at this critical turn in his life, Vivekananda suddenly became very pertinent. He became relevant, all of a sudden. The picture of the man that hung in their puja room suddenly floated into Ishaan's consciousness. His face was exceptionally handsome, with hair parted down the middle, gazing downwards. Ma loved that picture. She would wave incense at it every morning and evening. Baba would smirk. He was a communist. But he never came between Ma and her devotion to Vivekananda. Ishaan had literally grown up listening to stories about Vivekananda from Ma. About how he swam the ocean at Kanyakumari and attained enlightenment atop the rock that now bears his name. About how he went over to the New World and preached Hinduism. Or Vedanta. Advaita Vedanta, to be more precise. Ishaan loved all of this when he was a child. But as he had grown up so had the distance between him and Vivekananda. He drifted more towards Baba and his gospel of rationality and atheism as he grew up into adulthood. Baba had taught him to reason, and never accept anything at face value. He began to dislike this 'exceptionally handsome escapist', as Baba called Vivekananda. *Ghar chora mahapurush.* But now, all of a sudden, the distance between him and this handsome escapist began to narrow, pressed on by the weight of events. If nothing, there was strength in his utterances. Strength, he now badly needed.

Ishaan looked up at the sky. The clouds went on drifting in it, as before. Human predicament made no difference to them. They were as heartless as the mountains, where they went to empty themselves of their life, like Kamikaze pilots on suicide missions. Ishaan turned at Uma. She was staring at the mountains, her hand fiddling with the Rudraksha bead around her neck. She was whispering something. Ishaan listened carefully. It was a Sanskrit hymn of Siva …

Karpur Gauram Karunavatarm
Sansar Saram Bhujagendra Haram
Sada Vasantam Hridayare Vrinde
Bhavam Bhavami Sahitam Namami

Ishaan couldn't take it anymore. He felt as if someone was beating his head with a baton. He yelled at her, "Are you insane! People are dying all around you, and in this charnel pit you are taking the name of Siva! What has he done for you? You nearly died in the plane crash … and you are slowly dying now in this bloody cold … and to top it all, there are man-eating leopards prowling about for fucks sake!"

Uma looked straight into his eyes and answered, "What better place to take Siva's name than in a charnel pit?"

Ishaan felt like tearing his hair off in frustration and rage. He simply bumped his fist against the metal floor. It made a loud thud. But his aggression made no difference to Uma. She kept staring at him, her eyes fixed in her conviction. Then she slowly answered, "See … when I was born, my parents found out that I was *mangalik*, so they married me off to Siva when I was barely five … they also named me Uma for that very reason." She looked calmly at Ishaan and said, "So you see … nothing can happen to me. I am Siva's wife. He'll protect me, wherever I am. I trust him with all my life."

Ishaan was dumbfounded. He remembered something. Richard Dawkins perhaps. He had written somewhere that if one person hallucinates, it's madness. But when many people hallucinate, it's called Religion. Ishaan couldn't even laugh at the ludicrousness of the situation. It was too tragic to be funny.

"Ah … my head …" it was Richard. He was beginning to wake up. The two quickly rushed to his side. Ishaan came close to Richard's face and said, "I'm right here, buddy … right here," as he patted his head. "Are you alright?"

Richard didn't answer.

"Bring me the bottle of vodka," Ishaan said to Uma.

Uma looked around for the bottle, found it and brought it to Ishaan. Ishaan quickly poured some of the liquid into Richard's mouth, prying his lips open with his fingers. Richard gulped down the vodka and slowly opened his eyes. The first thing he said was, "Where is she?"

Ishaan couldn't answer him. He looked at Uma. Uma looked Ishaan in the eye and then she turned them towards Richard. She sat down near him and slowly said, "Richard, she is not here anymore …"

Richard looked straight at her with disbelief and rage. Thank god he was tied up. Uma continued, "She has gone away to a better place, to be with her child … you must accept that."

Richard closed his eyes tight. Tears started pouring out of them, streaming down his cheeks and wetting his jacket. It was a good sign, thought Ishaan. Then he burst out into a wail. Ishaan and Uma waited for him, waited for him to cry off his insanity. After a while, he regained his composure.

Ishaan looked straight into his eyes and said, "Get a hold of the truth now … we've got to escape this hellhole … they're not coming to get us … so prepare yourself."

Richard stared back into his eyes. There was no sorrow in them. There was no rage in them. There was no madness in them. There was nothing in them, no emotions. Nothing. It was a blank stare. The kind Ishaan had seen in the eyes of the corpses he dissected during his college days. This man had lost his reason for existing. He was dead, for all intents and purposes. Ishaan understood him perfectly.

"Now get up," Ishaan called out to Richard while untying him.

Richard slowly got up and looked around himself for a while. Then he said, "Give me the booze," while he looked at Ishaan. Ishaan took the bottle from Uma's hand and handed it over to Richard. Within a few seconds, Richard emptied the entire bottle and dashed it against the metal floor. The bottle cracked into smithereens, the glass jumping off all around. Uma jumped with a start, clinging to Ishaan's shoulders, clasping them with her hands. Ishaan calmed her down with a wave of his hand and looked straight at Richard. He was preparing himself, without even noticing the two of them. He untied and then tightly tied up his shoelaces and picked up his backpack. He gathered whatever he could salvage and put them in his backpack, without even saying a word.

Ishaan got the cue. He said to Uma, "Let's get ready." And then he proceeded to do the same as Richard. Uma followed suit. The three salvaged whatever they could. Richard had finished first. He snapped at the two, "What are you waiting for … let's crack on," and waded into the snow. They were doing it. If civilization didn't come to them, they had to go to civilization. *If the mountain doesn't come to Muhammad, Muhammad must go to the mountain.* The three left their shelter and ventured into the unknown.

They had walked for miles in the blinding whiteness of the snow. It was surreal. Wherever you looked, there was snow, with only the mountain peaks for reference. They followed the slope of the mountain and kept on walking. They didn't know where they were going. But they knew that they were going down. That was all they wanted to do. Just keep climbing down. Maybe, after a day's journey, they just might find a sleepy little village at the foot of the mountains. That would be paradise. And it was better to walk during the day, cause during the night they would be vulnerable to the attacks of the leopards. Uma kept the kukri close to her hand. Just in case. Richard and Ishaan both had broken steel rods. They served as walking sticks as well. The three trekked down the mountain all day, stopping twice to catch their breath or to urinate. Uma had no privacy. Privacy was a luxury that she couldn't afford up here. Whenever they felt thirsty, they gulped down some vodka. They hadn't eaten or drunk anything but vodka for the past one day. At this point, even their sweat smelled of alcohol.

Towards evening, they hit vegetation. The snowy whiteness of the mountain had given way to some greenery. They could spot trees at a distance. Pines. Nothing else could grow at this altitude. The sun had completed three-quarters of its journey around the sky. The three had stopped to catch their breaths when they caught sight of the greenery. They were on a ridge in the mountains. There was a deep fall to their left, while to the right there was a slope. Uma sat on a slab of stone. Ishaan stood midway between her and Richard. Richard was in the front. Uma took off her backpack and panted. Richard yelled at her, "Come on, time is of the essence." That man was now as practical as the slab of stone that she was sitting on right now. Ishaan too felt like dropping his backpack to the ground and resting a while, when suddenly Richard exclaimed, "Hey … look out!" and ran towards Uma.

Ishaan quickly turned in her direction. What he saw froze him to the ground. Two full-grown snow leopards were prancing towards her. They were running effortlessly on the snow. They were about thirty metres away from her back and approaching fast. Uma turned around and fell to the ground. Richard ran up to her, picked her up from the snow, helped her to her feet and pushed her away towards Ishaan. Uma ran to him and hid behind his back. Ishaan yelled at Richard, "Run, man, run. Run for your life!" as he picked up pace.

Richard turned his head towards Ishaan, looked straight into his eyes, pointed his right index finger at him and said, "You run … I'm already dead."

Ishaan suddenly saw life in his eyes. Such life he had never seen before. There was a rainbow of emotions in his gaze. There was rage. There was sorrow. And, by God, there was love. The desire for getting reunited with his wife. His eyes burned like a lamp nearing death. There is a burst of life and light, before the final darkness. This was suicide. Richard dropped his backpack onto the ground and clenched his right fist into a punch; all the while the leopards were gaining in on him. He turned in their direction and just as the first leopard pounced on him, he punched at it. Ishaan couldn't tell whether it was Richard's hand or the leopard's skull but something cracked. He distinctly heard a cracking noise. The leopard reeled back and fell to the ground. The other leopard pounced on him. He caught it with both his hands and swung it over and threw it over the ridge, into the chasm on the left. This strength was superhuman. His loss had made him a berserker. In the meanwhile, the other leopard had recovered. It pounced on him, straight for the throat. Ishaan heard Richard yell out a blood-curdling cry. The leopard pinned him to the ground with its bite and was now mauling him. Richard was trying hard to rid himself of the leopard's bite, but its grip was like death. Blood. Blood flowed freely all around. It oozed fresh from Richard's wounds. It flowed like a river from his throat. Ishaan and Uma had been transfixed to their spots by the weight of the events unfolding right in front of their eyes. Richard was dying right in front of their eyes. Then, suddenly, Ishaan felt it. Helplessness suddenly changed to rage. He felt blood rushing into his brain and his muscles. His heart was pumping over-time. This was the fight or flight moment. Ishaan chose to fight. He yelled at Uma, "Give me the kukri!"

Uma was in a daze, her eyes fixed on where Richard lay, being mauled by the leopard. It took her a moment to recover. She hurriedly took out the kukri from underneath her clothes and gave it to Ishaan, her hands shaking. The naked blade in his hands made Ishaan feel alive. The barbaric blood of his hunter-gatherer ancestors danced up in his veins. His focus was completely on the leopard. He rushed towards it, the kukri gleaming in the light of the falling sun. He dashed straight at the leopard and started stabbing it wildly. The animal was busy with Richard. It couldn't react properly. The moment it was about to pounce on Ishaan, Richard held it back, with all his berserk might. Now it was Richard's turn to pin the animal down. He pinned it down with all his body while Ishaan kept on stabbing it with his kukri. He didn't count the number of times he stabbed it. But when he was finished, the leopard was dead and the kukri looked like Kali's tongue, dripping with fresh blood.

Ishaan let the kukri drop to the snow beneath. It fell onto the snow and dug into it, like Siva's phallus when he was cursed by the sages at the Deodar Forest. The snow sucked up the blood on it, lapping it up hungrily. Ishaan looked at Richard. He lay atop the leopard, his head buried in the leopard's stomach, his strong, muscular arms laying limp around the leopard's neck. Ishaan fell to Richard's position and turned him up. He was alive, barely. He was breathing with difficulty. His neck was torn open, fresh blood gushing out from it. Ishaan's eyes burned with the exertion and despair. Richard was dying right in front of his eyes and there was nothing, absolutely nothing that he could do to save him. He held Richard's hands tightly in his and took his head on his lap. Richard looked up at him, his eyes drifting towards infinity. "Ma ... te ..." he gurgled up blood.

"I'm here, mate!" Ishaan yelled, his eyes flooding with tears. Richard pointed his right index finger at Uma and then his hand dropped onto the snow. *A bright plumed bird flew away into the heavens, free at last.*

"Aaahhhh!" Ishaan screamed out loud. The stone-hearted mountains all around echoed his cry. A mockery, it seemed. Ishaan burst out crying. He cried like a baby. The camaraderie that he had struck with Richard flashed before his eyes, a succession of bright, detailed images. Their first drink. Their first laughter. Richard's bright face by the light of the bonfire. The scent of vodka on his breath. Their wrestling bout on the snow ... all left behind. The person had departed. What was left behind were his folded-up clothes, bloody and tattered.

Vaasamsi Jeernani Yathaa Vihayaa
Naavani Grihnaati Naroparaani
Thatha Shareeraani Vihayaa Jeernaa
Nyanyaani Samyaati Navaani Dehee

Uma slowly came up to him and sat by his side. A teardrop trickled down her lashes. It fell on the snow and sank in it. She checked herself. She had to look after Ishaan, who was crying himself hoarse like a baby. She felt affection for him. Her heart welled up with care and concern. She took Ishaan's head and put it on her breasts, hugging him tight. Ishaan put his hands around her shoulder and wept. She felt like the only woman in existence, who had to comfort the only man in existence. She let him weep.

Ishaan slowly looked up at Uma. Her face was ablaze with the light of the setting sun. He turned towards the horizon. The sun had turned orange. It would be only a matter of time before it turned red. They had to find shelter for the night. But they couldn't let Richard's body lie there. The two deftly dug up a grave in the snow for Richard, and carefully laid him in it. By this time they had gathered considerable experience in digging graves. They quickly covered the grave with snow. While digging, they found soil. The layer of snow was beginning to thin. There was hope that they might just make it. Ishaan checked Richard's backpack. There were two bottles of vodka in it, along with other things. He salvaged what was essential, like a flashlight and left what was not. He put one of the bottles atop Richard's grave. His tombstone.

The shadows began to lengthen as the two marched towards the Pines. And just as they entered the Pine forest, darkness fell. Ishaan quickly turned on the flashlight. The tops of the peaks still had light lingering on them. The flashlight guided them through the Pine forest. They came across a clearing. Ishaan heard the sound of running water. His heart jumped up with joy. Maybe there was a waterfall nearby. He looked at Uma and said, "Do you hear that?"

"Yes!"

"I'm going to check … you stay here with the stuff …" and he dropped his backpack on the ground.

"Don't be a smartass," Uma rebuked him. "Let me go … you are already too exhausted. I'll count so that you'll know my position."

Ishaan hesitated at first, but then he assented.

Uma took the flashlight from him and walked off in search of fresh water. "One … two … three …" her voice grew fainter and fainter as she waded into the dark.

Ishaan sat down on the ground. The snow was thinner here. He drew a smiley face on the snow with his fingers, almost scraping the soil underneath.

"… thirteen fourteen …" He could still hear her count. "Twenty … twenty one twenty two twenty three …"

Where was twenty four? Ishaan stood up, straining his ears. All he heard was the sound of the water. But no twenty four. He yelled, "Uma! Uma?" No answer. He was beginning to panic. He ran in the direction that she had gone, leaving all the things on the snow-covered ground.

Suddenly came her voice, "I'm here …"

It was not coming from very far away. Ishaan stopped running, "Did you find water?"

"Yes … and more … come and look. I'll count."

Ishaan quickly ran back to the smiley face and gathered the two backpacks.

"One two three …"

He followed her voice. It grew louder and louder. "… fourteen fifteen sixteen …"

Yes, he was coming closer. "Twenty five twenty six twenty seven …"

It was at thirty one that he found her. He sighed in relief.

"What did you find?" he asked her.

"Well, see for yourself," she said while pointing the flashlight towards something.

His eyes followed the beam of light and hit upon an opening. The mouth of a cave! The two slowly made their way into it, cautiously, Ishaan leading the way. Who knew what wild animal would be lying inside it? Ishaan took out his kukri. With the left hand he held up the flashlight and in the right one the kukri. The flashlight illuminated their path inside. Ishaan focused it on the ground, while slowly making his way inside. When suddenly, he saw something. A cat. A little white cat, slowly coming towards them, looking up at the light with beady eyes. No! It was not a cat. It was a leopard cub! Ishaan jumped up in shock. He quickly twisted the beam around the cave, jabbing the darkness with this sabre of light in his hands. No, there was not another living creature inside, except for this furry little rascal. The cub came up to them and started mewing. The first instinct that hit Ishaan's heart was compassion. Care. But it was pushed aside by the overwhelming hunger that he had been suppressing for two days. He quickly dropped the flashlight on the ground and picked up the cub in his hands.

Just when he was about to slice off its throat with the kukri, Uma screamed. "Are you insane!" And she snatched the cub away from his hands.

Ishaan looked up at her and said, "Are you not hungry?"

Uma paused then she said, "Yes, I am. I'm famished … but that is no reason to kill this innocent little cub!" So saying she started patting it.

"Innocent?" Ishaan felt scandalized, "It was probably the parents of this cub that killed Riley and Richard, and you want to protect it?"

"Yes!" Uma answered firmly.

There was no point arguing. All he knew at this point was the overwhelming hunger in his stomach. Richard and Riley's deaths were extra reasons. He didn't waste a word arguing with this fool. He snatched the cub right away from her hands and held up his kukri. Just as he was about to stab the cub with it, Uma held his hand with all her might, crying in terror. "Kill and eat me! Eat my meat … but spare this cub," she said, her voice choking with emotion.

Ishaan let the cub down on the ground. He was flabbergasted. This woman truly was insane. Why else would she risk her life for the life of a little leopard cub, a walking steak of meat! The cub came close to Uma and started rubbing its back against her legs. Maybe it was showing gratitude.

"Okay, know what? Fuck it! Where is the water?" he asked her as impolitely as he could.

"It's just outside, to the left," Uma answered, pointing out the direction with her finger.

Ishaan picked up the flashlight from the ground and dropped his backpack on the floor of the cave. He then went outside.

The soft light of the moon carpeted the snow under his feet. He looked up at the sky. The crescent had grown a bit. The moon was waxing. Stars twinkled around her face. They reminded Ishaan of his nursery rhyme book … the pictures in it were similar to the sight that now greeted him up in the sky.

Twinkle twinkle little star
How I wonder what you are?

Ishaan turned to the left, where the water gurgled against the rocks. He held up his flashlight. The outer layer of the waterfall had hardened into ice, but underneath the water flowed down free and fresh. Ishaan put the flashlight on the ground and lurched towards the water. He ran underneath the waterfall and cupped his hands. The cold, clear water filled up his palms. He drank the water greedily, slurping and rinsing it inside his mouth. Ah! Life. He kept drinking it, on and on and on. As he couldn't eat the leopard cub, he had to fill his belly with water. He had to quench his hunger as well as his thirst. Vodka seemed repulsive to him now. Its very smell would make him puke. So he drank.

When he had had his fill, Ishaan turned away from the water, wiping his lips with the back of his palms. He smacked his lips in satisfaction. He picked up the flashlight from the ground and turned it towards the trees. He spied some low-hanging twigs sticking out of the trees. He went towards them and jabbed them off with the kukri. He went on searching for firewood; jabbing off twigs and small branches from the Pines. When he was done, he bundled them together and put them under his arms. He carried them all back to the cave.

The flashlight illuminated his way inside. Uma was sitting near the entrance of the cave, running her hand over the fur of the leopard cub. The cub was asleep in her arms. She was staring out at the night sky. The soft radiance of the moon was playing with her features. She was humming a song. Ishaan listened closely. It was a Nepali love song.

Ali ora aau, maya basa merai cheu.
Jugai jane pirati lamla.
Baina rumal deu.
Jugai jane pirati lamla.
Baina rumal deu.

Ishaan kept looking at Uma. She didn't even notice him standing near her. Her mind and heart were now far away, far far away. Ishaan purposefully turned off the flashlight. "Young love," Ishaan whispered to himself. Who was she thinking about? Maybe someone back in Delhi, or perhaps a Nepali youth. Who could tell? He cleared his throat to draw her attention.

Uma looked at him, suddenly coming back to the mountains, to the cave, to the leopard cub, to him. She excused herself and drew in her legs, which had been blocking the entrance to the cave.

Ishaan went inside and dropped the firewood on the floor. He then turned on the flashlight and searched for his backpack. He opened it and took out the last remaining bottle of vodka. Smirnoff. He twisted open its cap and put the bottle near the firewood. Then he proceeded to heap some of the firewood together in the middle of the cave, saving the rest for later. The cave was not very big. He piled the firewood on the floor, poured in some vodka and took out his Zippo. "Come here," he said to Uma while lighting the fire. The flames caught up rapidly. The wood was dry and the vodka was strong. By the light of the fire, Ishaan looked around the cave. Yes, it was a medium-sized cave. Four hundred, five hundred square feet tops. Smaller than his flat in Delhi, but it was a shelter. A shelter that they now badly needed. Ishaan looked at the flames crunching away at the wood. They reminded him of the Dandaka Forest episode in the Mahabharata. Krishna and Arjuna had burned down the Dandaka Forest to make room for Indraprastha, or Delhi. Yes. That was the cost of civilization.

The fire warmed the chilly mountain air inside the cave. Ishaan felt comfortable. He looked at Uma, she was staring at him, still fiddling with the cub in her arms. The cub was still asleep. Their eyes locked. Ishaan moved his chin downwards slightly to make an inviting gesture with his head. Uma got up, carefully carrying the sleeping cub and came up to him. She sat down near the fire, putting the cub on a folded piece of cloth on the ground. Then she wrapped the cloth around it with motherly affection. Ishaan kept looking at all this with utmost attention. He sighed. "You're caring for that little furry devil as if it were your own child."

Uma looked straight up into his eyes and answered, "I value life."

"Whose life should you be valuing at this time, the cub's or yours?" Ishaan asked her straight up.

"See, Ishaan; it's not the cub's fault. You know that. Why should it suffer the consequences of the actions that it didn't commit? Killing it and eating it might make no difference to you, but if I did it, it would rob me of my sanity."

"I already doubt your sanity," Ishaan was pulling no punches.

Uma looked into his eyes with a startled gaze.

"Firstly, you keep clinging to that Rudraksha bead around your neck despite all that has happened. You keep ranting that you are Siva's wife, that he'll protect you. And you say that you study at JNU. Man, that place is the scrapyard of superstitions! Secondly, under the present circumstances, you should be worried sick about hunger. Have you eaten anything for the past two days? I'm sure you haven't, because neither have I. Because there is no food!" Ishaan's voice was rising to a yell; his hands spread out in the air as he gesticulated for added effect. "And you keep ranting that you value life, while the only life you should value right now is your own. Who do you think you are? Mother Teresa?" the veins in Ishaan's neck were bulging out in excitement.

Uma's eyes welled up. Two heavy beads of tear swam down from them and fell on the floor, glistening in the light of the fire. Rudra Aksha. She looked at Ishaan, her eyes literally begging him to apologize. But she couldn't say that. There was a lump in her throat which she could neither swallow nor throw up.

Suddenly, Ishaan felt pity for her. She was completely helpless up here without him. This young Nepali girl, who had suffered with him. Who had made it this far. Ishaan felt it his duty to protect her, care for her and love her. He should be her pillar of strength at this difficult hour. Instead, he was scolding her. Sure, she had her shortcomings, as he had his. But this was not the moment to chastise. It was the moment to comfort and care. Ishaan calmed down and looked into her eyes, his gaze softening to make an apology, "Listen, Uma," Ishaan cleared his throat, "I'm sorry. Don't cry. It's just that I'm too worked up right now. Please, forgive me. I didn't mean to hurt you."

Uma covered her mouth with her palms and broke into a muffled cry. Ishaan bent over to touch her and comfort her. At his touch, Uma slid into his arms and held his shoulders. She put her head on his chest and started crying.

Ishaan held her tightly to his chest and patted her head. He felt sorry for her. He really did. For the first time since *her,* he had felt that way for another woman. "Don't cry … I'm sorry. I really am," he whispered into her ears.

"You men are all the same … all of you!" she complained, wiping her nose with her sleeve, "You never understand us women … you only hurt us."

Ishaan smiled. Oh, he understood women alright. All they need is a good hump. That's all. That's the way of Nature. Women are built that way, with wide hips and heavy breasts. To lure men into having sex with them and bearing children. That's their purpose. All but one of them … *her. She* was 'the woman'. Without comparison. *Ekam Evadwitiyam.* The rest were just fuckdolls in his eyes.

Uma looked up at him and said, "You said you have a girlfriend. Do you treat her this way too, as you treated me?" There was curiosity and jealousy in her eyes.

Ishaan read her gaze carefully. Then slowly he held her away from his chest and looked away at the walls of the cave. Uma looked intently at his face. His eyes were starting to water. Was it the heat of the fire? Or was it something else? She wondered. Then Ishaan turned towards her and without looking into her eyes said, "I lied."

"About what?" Uma asked, bewildered.

"About my girlfriend."

"Did she leave you?" Uma was all ears.

"No. She died."

Uma was absolutely silent.

"Her name was Fahima … Fahima Mirza. We had been together since our school days," Ishaan's eyes were brimming with tears. Yet he held them back with great effort.

"What happened?" Uma couldn't stop herself from asking.

"She was pregnant … with our first child. We were supposed to run away and get married. It had all been arranged. She would wait for me under the Qutub Minar, where we had our first kiss. I was supposed to pick her up from there. But something terrible happened …" he sniffed, "… there was an accident. A car crash. My parents were severely injured. Prakash, my buddy, called me up. My *Mashi* had called him to tell him about the accident since she couldn't reach me. I rushed immediately to the hospital … but … they passed away!" Ishaan let out his first sob, "I was so caught up with all of this that I didn't even notice the eighty nine missed calls on my phone. She had been calling me continuously. I had left the phone in my car. She waited there, under the Qutub Minar, for eight long, gruelling hours, uncertain and worried sick about me. She had all her bags packed. She was ready to embark on married life with me … her eyes were filled with these dreams. Finally, she gave up. She must have thought that I had cheated her. Deceived her. Made a mockery of her innocent affections. She must have felt cheated …" Ishaan stopped at this point, almost blind with tears, his voice quivering with emotions.

He turned towards Uma and finally breaking down he somehow said, "She drowned herself … in the Yamuna …" his voice trailing off into a loud wail.

Uma looked at Ishaan, her eyes welling up as well. He needed her right now. He needed comfort. He needed a shoulder to cry on. He needed someone to share the weight of his sorrow. Someone to be with him. Someone he could rely on … forever. At that very moment, she offered herself to him. She was his, if only he would care to take her as his woman. Her past melted away in his tears. Her future lay in his arms. She was his … yes, she was his, forever and ever and ever. She bent forward to hug him. Ishaan didn't even notice her. She came closer, opened her jacket, and exposed the soft sweater underneath. Her bosom was ready to receive him. She took Ishaan's head in her hands and laid it on her bosom. Ishaan grabbed her shoulder and cried piteously. She bent her head forward and kissed his lips. Ishaan wasn't prepared for this. He was taken aback. But, just as suddenly, he felt all warm inside. He was beginning to heat up and it was not just the fire. She was his for the taking, and he knew it. He kissed her. They locked lips passionately and kissed. She began undressing him and he began undressing her. The fire cast long shadows of the two on the walls of the cave. Soon the shadows reclined on each other, tearing open the coverings over their flesh, their bare, naked flesh. The leopard cub slept as peacefully as before. Now it had a father.

AJNA

"Ishaaan!" Ishaan jumped to his feet. He was butt naked. He had fallen asleep after making love to Uma. His clothes were heaped on the floor of the cave, near where they had slept. He looked at his wrist. There was something on it that had not been there earlier. It was her Rudraksha bead. She had tied it around his right wrist, before going out of the cave. Her scream was coming from the outside. Suddenly there came another noise, a loud growl. It was coming from just outside the cave. Ishaan madly searched for his kukri. It was lying on the floor, near the little leopard cub. It was still asleep. Ishaan grabbed it and ran out into the cold outside, butt naked. This was it!

What Ishaan saw outside amazed and enraged him beyond measure. The other leopard, which Richard had thrown over the ridge hadn't died. It had somehow managed to cling on to its life. It had somehow made its way back to the cave. It was its home. And they had been occupying it without its permission. It had come to reclaim its cave and its cub. Uma must have gone out on some business, probably to take a piss, when the bastard had attacked her. Ishaan saw that it had pinned Uma to the ground with its forelegs. No, it wasn't mauling her. It was waiting … for the man of the house. It was waiting for him.

The pussy was pissed. It would be a fight between them, mano a mano. Everything else hung in the balance.

Ishaan bent forward a little, the kukri in his hand bleeding moonlight, and he walked towards the leopard. On seeing him it let go of Uma and slowly started moving in a circle. Ishaan followed suit, every single muscle in his body pumped up with adrenaline, his sinews twitching with anticipation. He felt everything keenly. The chilly mountain air, the soft radiance of the moon, the twinkling stars, the sound of the waterfall. It wasn't fear that grabbed his heart, but a heightened sense of things. He felt everything, yet he didn't feel a thing. The two began circling each other, their eyes locked. This was the dance of death. It was a battle of nerves. Ishaan forgot everything … who he was, where he was, he forgot Fahima and he forgot Uma. The only thing that mattered to him now was those two glowing eyes circling him, looking out for his every single movement. One false step and it would all be over. The whole Universe began to whirl away into nothingness. The mountains, the moon, the stars, Uma … everything dissolving away into those two glowing, roving eyes. His whole sanity now depended on the kukri in his hand, held up and ready. It was the kukri that was pegging him down to sanity, to life. And then, just as suddenly, the eyes leapt up towards him. Ishaan was ready. The kukri tore into the leopard's flesh. The animal growled out in pain and rage and madly jabbed at him with its right paw. Ishaan ducked. He took out the kukri from its flesh and put it in again, harder. He stabbed again and again and again. The leopard attacked him with his left paw, its nails digging into his flesh. Pain wasn't a luxury he could afford right now. He held away the left paw with his left hand and went on stabbing wildly. The leopard again flung its right paw at him. Ishaan ducked again. He kneeled down, let go of the animal's left paw and held its belly with his left hand, his right one busily stabbing the animal to death. The leopard growled out in pain and madly flung both its paws where Ishaan's head should have been. But it wasn't there. It was at the level of its belly. Ishaan went on stabbing. The feeling was orgasmic. Finally, he dug the kukri deep into the leopard's abdomen and tore out its intestines. The blood gushed out, fresh and warm. It seeped down the kukri and onto Ishaan's hand. Ishaan dug the kukri even deeper and swiped it upwards with all his strength. The animal cried out in horrible pain as the kukri tore through the entire length of its belly. Ishaan brought the kukri up to the animal's neck, slicing everything that stood in the way. Ishaan now felt what Richard had felt when he was fighting the leopards. The power and the pleasure. The sensation filled his entire body, from the tips of the hair on his head to the nails on his toes. He had gone berserk. Finally, he dug the kukri even deeper, this time into the animal's head from inside its neck. It made one final attempt at resistance. With both its paws it dug into Ishaan's back. But Ishaan didn't feel anything at this point. He was bleeding ecstasy. Then with one final upward jab, the kukri tore into the animal's brain and broke through its skull. The paws fell away and the animal limped over Ishaan. Its mouth was near his left ear. The animal made a strange sound, "Soham! Soham! Soham!" And then all was silent.

The water began falling again; the moon began shining again, and the stars began twinkling again. The world came back to Ishaan. He dropped the kukri along with the leopard that was staked to it through the head and looked at Uma. She was lying unconscious in the snow. Her left leg was bleeding. The leopard must have bit her leg while pinning her down. He didn't feel his pain. It was her pain that really mattered. He went over and took her up in his arms and brought her back to the cave. The fire was smouldering now. No extra firewood was left. She must have put it all into the fire before going out. She wanted to keep him warm. He laid her down by the sleeping cub. By the light of the smouldering fire, he looked for the bottle of vodka. It was near his clothes. He took it up and poured some of the liquid onto her wound. She didn't make a noise. Ishaan put his hand to her nose. Yes, she was breathing. Now he felt it, the pain. He bit his lips and contorted his face to suppress it. He quickly doused himself with the vodka. The pain jumped up a notch, before settling down to bearable levels. His thought turned to Uma. Must keep her warm. Must get firewood. Where was the kukri? It was outside, sticking out of the dead animal's head. He went outside.

The animal was lying in the snow. Its blood had coloured the snow pink. Ishaan put his right hand into the animal's neck and searched for the handle of the kukri. He found it and started pulling at it. It was stuck. He pulled at it harder, his face getting red and contorted. By God! He must have inherited Richard's strength when he fought the beast. He had put the kukri into its head but had a hard time pulling it out. Finally, after some serious exertion, the kukri came out. Blood and brains were sticking to it. A slimy red slush flowed down to his hand. Ishaan rubbed it off against the animal's fur, wiping the kukri clean. He was feeling hungry all over again. The hunger was unbearable. An idea came to him. He could eat the leopard! Yes! He would eat the leopard. But first, he must gather firewood. He went to the pines again and sliced off low-hanging twigs and branches with the kukri. He gathered whatever could be burnt. He brought them all back to the cave and put them on the smouldering fire and added some vodka. The fire crackled up. He went outside again. He sat on the snow, bent over the leopard and started skinning it. This was vengeance. He was taking revenge for Riley, for Richard and for Uma. He would skin it, eat its meat and wear its skin. And what was more, he would sleep in its cave, with its cub sleeping by his side. Ishaan whistled in satisfaction. Revenge couldn't get any better than this!

I am monarch of all I survey,
My Right there is none to dispute
From the centre all round to the sea,
I am lord of the fowl and the brute.

Ishaan deftly skinned the dead animal, his dissection skills coming to ample usage. He then wore the skin around his waist, tying it up like a skirt. The skin dripped fresh blood. Ishaan's eyes glittered with animalistic pleasure. He then dragged the skinless animal into the cave. The fire was burning. He sliced off a portion of its breast with the kukri and held it out into the fire, using the kukri as a fork. The fire crackled on the meat and slowly began cooking it. The scent of burnt meat filled the air within the cave. It was perhaps the most appetizing smell he had ever smelt in all his life! His mouth began to water. Ishaan couldn't wait. He quickly put the half-cooked meat into his mouth and chewed. The juices splattered onto his taste buds. He closed his eyes in pleasure. It was orgasmic. Oh, heaven, heaven, heaven! He went on chewing, enjoying every single bite. This was his first meal in two days and he relished every moment of it. He went on slicing, cooking and chewing the meat till he had had his fill. There was still a lot of meat left. It would serve them for an entire week. He looked at Uma. She was still unconscious. She could eat when she woke up. He went over to her and sat by her side, gently patting her head. His clothes were nearby. He brought his jacket and put it over her and tucked a sweater under her head. Let her rest, he thought.

He sat there, near Uma, staring at the fire. The crackling flames giving him company. Should he sleep? No, he couldn't sleep … not after all this. He had to stay awake. He had to protect her, in case another leopard showed up. He couldn't take any chance. He kept the kukri ready near his hand. Thoughts drifted in and out of his head. What did he learn from all of this? What was the purpose of all of this? Is there any purpose at all? Or is Life pure chance? Nothing but a blind roll of the dice. What was Life really about, what was the meaning of all of it …?

Suddenly he felt someone approaching. Someone or something was walking towards the cave. He couldn't put a finger on how he knew this, but he felt it, in his guts. Sixth sense? Bullshit! There is no such thing. But he kept the kukri ready. Suddenly the moon cast a shadow at the entrance of the cave. Someone was really coming. The shadow was that of a human being. Ishaan strained his eyes and looked at it. Just as suddenly, the person entered. The light from the fire fell on the person's face … it was *her!* It was Fahima.

SAHASRARA

Ishaan's eyes bulged out in amazement and disbelief. He sat there dumbfounded, unable to comprehend anything. His grip on reality was loosening, slipping through his fingers like sand. *She* entered the cave and stood at the entrance. *She* was completely naked. *Her* hair flowing down to *her* hips; *her* plump breasts hanging from *her* chest. *She* smiled at him. It was the most bewitching smile ever. Ishaan's jaw dropped in amazement. Was he dreaming? Was he hallucinating? He pinched himself. Yes, he was awake. Then who was this person standing in front of him. *She* had died. He knew it. *She* gently came over to him and bent down, *her* breasts touching his face. Yes. He knew this touch. He intimately knew this touch. *She* undid the skin he was wearing around his waist, flinging it open with both hands. Then *she* touched his penis. *Her* touch worked like magic. He was feeling it. The old memories rushed into his mind, flooding him with delight. She tugged at his legs with her hands and spread them wide open. Ishaan did nothing to stop her. Then she sat down upon him, adjusting his phallus with one hand so that it entered her vagina. Then, she began the ritual of intimacy, never speaking a single word. Her smile did all the talking.

She held his shoulder with her hands and continued the intercourse. Up and down, up and down. Over and over again. Ishaan did nothing. Absolutely nothing. He let go of everything. He stopped resisting. She didn't belong to him. He belonged to her. He let go. He just closed his eyes in delight, absolute delight. Her rhythmic movement on his body made him go mad with ecstasy. He put his two arms backwards against the floor of the cave for support. He didn't even hold her. How long did their coitus last, he couldn't tell. But just as he was about to ejaculate, she grabbed his phallus, holding it tightly so that the semen did not rush out. Then she got off him and let go of his phallus. She cupped her palms so as to gather the semen in them. Ishaan emptied himself in her palms. Oh God! The pleasure, the pleasure, the pleasure! She smeared the semen on his forehead. Then she just said, "It is done." Words cannot describe the music that was there in her voice! Ishaan opened his eyes slowly. Her smiling face greeted him. Ishaan kept looking as she got up and turned away towards the mouth of the cave. He kept on looking as her figure walked away from him, one step at a time. Finally, she disappeared into the night.

Ishaan fell back on the floor, quaking with bliss. He lay there like that for a long time. He didn't sleep. He just lay on the cold, hard floor of the cave, drunk with bliss. There were no thoughts in his mind. Absolutely nothing. He knew just one thing and one thing only. He existed. He was aware of that. And he was blissful. *Sat. Chit. Ananda.* Who was that woman who came and had sexual intercourse with him was not that important at this moment. The only thing was that this moment existed. Ishaan was acutely aware of that very moment. His whole being was filled with indescribable peace and blessedness. It wasn't Fahima who had come to him at the very crux of his existence on the planet; it was *Mahamaya* Herself who had come in the guise of Fahima. She had come to give him the Ultimate Pleasure,

Paramananda. And in return she took all his emptiness away, filling him to his fingertips with bliss. Ishaan had read somewhere that the *Kundalini shakti* residing in every individual is feminine. In the rarest of the rare cases, the kundalini takes the form of a woman and consorts with the yogi, copulates with him and grants him Enlightenment.

After a while, when he came back to normal consciousness, Ishaan got up and looked at Uma. She was sleeping peacefully like a child. She was too tired even to feel the pain of the wound on her ankle. Ishaan went out of the cave, tying the leopard skin tightly around his waist. He didn't feel the cold. As a matter of fact, he felt nothing at all; only an unspeakable bliss filled his entire being. He looked at the moon. It was a crescent adorning the forehead of the vast mountain in front of him. The whiteness of the mountain and its sheer beauty were enhanced a thousandfold by the moonlight. Ishaan smiled a beatific smile. This smile was one of complete realization. Shakti completed Shiva. *She* completed him. He had to become completely empty so that he might be filled to the brim. Yes, he was empty now, completely empty. Hence, he was completely full now. *Shunyavam Purnamam*. That which is empty is full. Everything that had happened to him made sense now. All that pain, all that misfortune, that entire struggle. Everything had been rewarded. A feeling of thankfulness arose from the very depths of his being and sped towards the heavens above. No, he was not thanking God. There was no such thing as God. He was simply thanking himself, thanking himself for his sheer tenacity, for the fact that he held on after so many failures, so much pain and such great misfortunes.

Ishaan felt like dancing. He leapt up and swirled around. It was the most effortless action that he had done ever. He danced and danced and danced, his every step exploding the earth with bliss. Ishaan was filled to the tips of his fingers with bliss and an unparalleled sense of completeness. He never knew he could dance in this fashion. The rhythm of his being was now synchronized with the rhythm of the Cosmos, so every action which he took felt effortless.

Uma was awakened by the sound of Ishaan's feet thumping on the ground. She slowly came out of the cave and was greeted by an awesome sight. Ishaan was wearing the leopard skin and he was dancing a supreme dance of ecstasy. The whole Universe was being reflected in his being. It was as if the entire Universe had incarnated in Ishaan's body and was now dancing a wild dance of bliss, the most graceful dance as well. The stars above, the mountain around, everything, everything was reflected in Ishaan's being. Ishaan had become the Universe and the Universe had become Ishaan. The pot had burst, uniting the space within with the vast recesses of the Universe. Uma knelt at the entrance of the cave, feeling helpless with amazement and devotion for Ishaan.

The next morning Uma woke up to find Ishaan sitting outside the entrance of the cave on a slab of rock. She went to him and sat at his feet, staring into the very depths of his eyes. The glance that she received was beatific. There was love and blissfulness in his eyes. Wherever his glance fell, nature blossomed. The pale lifeless gaze of his eyes had completely melted away to reveal an entirely new man. Uma didn't know this man and yet she knew him most intimately. "What are you thinking about?" Uma hesitantly asked Ishaan.

"Nothing … nothing at all. I feel no inclination to think about anything."

Uma paused a while and then began, "What happened to you last night? Why were you dancing?" while fully anticipating his answer.

Ishaan looked straight into Uma's eyes and answered, "I was dancing out of love."

"Love of what?" Uma asked.

"You and everything that there is," Ishaan stood up and went a few steps in front and turned around and said, "She came to me last night. Fahima came to me last night. She made me whole; she made me complete," he paused and then began, "I understand that it is difficult for you to understand, but I'll explain. Everything that has happened to us, has been for a purpose— has been due to our Karma. Every strife and every suffering has hammered our existence to perfection. We needed to be completely empty … I needed to be completely empty, and when we become completely empty, we become full; we become whole. The whole world is running about trying to be complete, trying to be whole. Every action that an individual takes is an effort to complete himself.

An individual goes out to watch a movie because she feels that watching the movie would make her whole, that it would fill up an empty place in her heart or that buying this item or that item would make her whole. That's why she buys it. But once she has bought that item her heart pines for another item which she then again feels would make her whole. But wholeness always eludes us. One must understand that completeness is not outside us, it is within. The trick is to become completely empty, just as we are right now. When we are completely empty, not only physically but also emotionally and spiritually, is when we become complete, whole." Ishaan looked at Uma. She was staring at him with amazement with her mouth wide open. He moved toward her and sat on the rock again. After a brief pause, he began again, "See, Uma, that is *Purna*," he said while pointing to the sky above, and then he said, "This is *Purna*," pointing to himself. "When *Purna* is taken away from *Purna, Purna* alone remains. *Om Purnamadah Purnam-Idam Purnaat Purnam Udachyate; Purnasya Purnamadaya Purnemeva Vishisishyate Om Shanti Shanti Shanti.* Last night was the night I became complete; I became whole. I've had the taste of *Paramananda* and hence I know what *Paramartha* is. I have no desires or disgust anymore, for I have realized who I am." Then he took a pause and finally said, "I am Siva, Sivoham. Sivoham." A silent and highly pregnant moment passed by as the two stared into each other's eyes.

Finally, Uma bowed her head and then joined her palms in adulation. Then she said, "I knew it. Last night when you were dancing, I felt as if the Universe had become you, and that you had become the Universe. The stars, the mountains, the forest, everything, everything was reflected in your being."

After a moment of brief pause, Uma asked Ishaan, "How do you see the world now? How does the world appear to you now that you have found Enlightenment?"

Ishaan took a wide sweep of the forest and mountains with his glance and then looked at Uma and said, "The whole of Creation is a constant Leela between Siva and Shakti. Siva is always passive while Shakti is always active. Look at the mountains around us. They are silent and meditative like Siva. Now, look at the light of the Sun falling on them. It is Shakti. It is not that the Mountains never existed. They always existed, but it is only with the aid of Shakti, the light of the Sun, that we can see them. The mountains come into being in our eyes only when the light of the sun is reflected from their snowy surface. Such is the case with the entire Universe. The Universe comes into being only when Siva interacts with Shakti. Siva has always existed. It is Shakti who reveals Siva to us. The Universe is Siva, while Shakti is the Power of Siva which reveals Siva to us."

"But is Siva not a God who lives in Mount Kailas?" Uma interjected.

Ishaan calmly looked at her and said, "There is no such thing as God. Siva is the archetypal Yogi; he is the highest Yogi, the gold standard of a Yogi. He is what a Yogi becomes when he has attained the highest of all knowledge, the knowledge of the Self. When I said I am Siva, I didn't mean that I have become a God; I simply meant that I have attained the highest attainment that a yogi could achieve. I have attained *Kaivalya*."

"What is *Kaivalya*?" Uma asked. Ishaan paused, and then slowly he began, "It is an indescribable feeling. It is the highest attainment. It is a feeling that nothing matters anymore. All has been achieved; there is no need to do anything anymore. It is the feeling of being completely one with the Universe. It is as if I have indeed become the entire Universe, and the Universe has become me. It is the feeling that nothing exists in the whole of Creation which is not me. I am me, you are me and so is the leopard cub inside the cave. The mountains are me, the rivers are me, the forest is me, the stars are me, the moon is me and so is the vast emptiness of the skies. All is me. Everything exists in me and I exist in everything."

The two sat silently for some time, absorbing the beauty that surrounded them. In those silent moments, Uma could intensely feel her longing for Ishaan as well as his love for her. She didn't care that Ishaan had realized himself. She only cared whether he loved her or not. Uma hesitantly asked Ishaan, "Will you marry me?"

Ishaan looked at her and said, "Let's marry," with a wonderful smile playing on his lips. Uma could die a thousand deaths and be born again just for that beautiful smile.

She blushed, stood up and went inside the cave. Ishaan kept sitting on the rock. After a while, Uma came out and said, "We can marry by mutual consent since there is no one to bear witness to our marriage."

Ishaan replied, "Let's marry the Gandharva way then, by mutual consent." Uma smiled. That evening, by the light of the bonfire and taking *Agni* as their witness, Ishaan married Uma and took her as his wife, while Uma took Ishaan as her husband. At night they consummated their marriage.

The two felt like they were the only man and wife in existence. No one else mattered. No one clsc existed. Just the two of them. They felt like Siva and Parvati sharing the solitude of the mountains between them. Ishaan had realized everything that there was to realize. He got the purpose of his life. And that purpose was *ananda*, bliss, happiness. What good is the life of a man if he has everything but happiness? And what better than the life of a man who has nothing but happiness? The root was pleasure, *ananda*. The Ultimate Meaning, *Paramartha* was the same as the Ultimate Pleasure, *Paramananda*. They were inseparable from each other, like fire and heat. *Paramartha* was Siva and *Paramanada* was Shakti. They were the obverse and reverse faces of the same coin. There was pleasure in Life and there was pleasure in Death. And there was pleasure in everything in between. What did Richard feel when he sacrificed his life for the two of them? What did he feel when he risked his life for Uma? The answer was pleasure. Happiness. *Ananda*. It was pleasure that moved the Universe. It was the beginning, the middle and the end of everything. Happiness was the incentive for all of our actions. No one would budge an inch if there was no incentive for happiness. And the root of that happiness was inside of us, and not outside. If happiness has to take the aid of external props, it wasn't happiness at all, it was slavery. The only happiness that was real was the one having its roots deep inside our being, in the very core of our existence. And Ishaan had found out the source of that happiness, and hence he was ever blissful. To be Full, one first has to become Empty. To be *Purna*, he first had to be *Shunya*. He had become *Shunya*, hence *she* filled him up. He was now *Purna*. Complete.

The two decided to rest awhile in the embrace of the mountains. The cave was a perfect home for them. They would share the solitude of their mountain home with each other. There was no hustle and bustle of human civilization up here in the mountains. As a matter of fact, the two had no need for the hustle and bustle of human civilization. They had all they wanted; each other. Ishaan waited till Uma had regained her health. He waited for her to recover. He waited for three days. In the meantime, they ate up all the meat they could and drank the water from the waterfall to their fill. They were properly rested and rehydrated by the third day. On the morning of the fourth day, he picked Uma up in his arms and the little leopard cub on his shoulder. But he didn't pick up any of their belongings. There was no need to. That life was over. He started journeying down the mountain. He walked and walked and walked. He walked the entire day and by afternoon he spied a sleepy little village at the foot of the mountain. He didn't stop. By evening, as the temple bells were ringing, he entered the village. The villagers were astounded to see this man, wearing a leopard skin and carrying this woman in his arms, with a leopard cub at his heels. They flocked in droves to see him, and they fell prostrate at his feet. Ishaan didn't even notice them. He kept standing there, with Uma in his arms, drunk with *bliss*. It was as if they made no difference to him. Their devotion or their derision was of no value to him. The world, as we perceive it, had fallen away from his eyes, revealing the essence of the Cosmos. And that essence was *Ananda*. Ishaan waded his way through the crowd of his devotees and made his way to the village temple. He looked in at the sanctum sanctorum of the temple. There was a *Shivling* inside. He put Uma down on the floor of the temple. She made him sit near her. He sat to the right and Uma sat to his left.

The villagers ran towards the two and fell at their feet, chanting "Om Namah Shivay!" The whole village rang out with the name of Siva. Then someone said, "Jay Uma Shankar!" *Victory to Uma Shankar.* Uma smiled, but Ishaan ... was silent. His eyes were far away, looking into the mountains. Uma had been right all along. The Man in the mountains did save her ... and that Man was Ishaan.

Om Namah Sivay

EPILOGUE

Manobuddhyahaṅkāra cittāni nāhaṃ
Na ca śrotrajihve na ca ghrāṇanetre
Na ca vyoma bhūmir na tejo na vāyuḥ
Cidānandarūpaḥ śivo'ham śivo'ham
Na ca prāṇasaṅjño na vai pañcavāyuḥ
Na vā saptadhātur na vā pañcakośaḥ
Na vākpāṇipādau na copasthapāyu
Cidānandarūpaḥ śivo'ham śivo'ham
Na me dveṣarāgau na me lobhamohau
Mado naiva me naiva mātsaryabhāvaḥ
Na dharmo na cārtho na kāmo na mokṣaḥ
Cidānandarūpaḥ śivo'ham śivo'ham
Na puṇyaṃ na pāpaṃ na saukhyaṃ na duḥkhaṃ
Na mantro na tīrthaṃ na vedā na yajña
Nhaṃ bhojanaṃ naiva bhojyaṃ na bhoktā
Cidānandarūpaḥ śivo'ham śivo'ham
Na me mṛtyuśaṅkā na me jātibhedaḥ
Pitā naiva me naiva mātā na janmaḥ
Na bandhur na mitraṃ gururnaiva śiṣyaḥ
Cidānandarūpaḥ śivo'ham śivo'ham
Ahaṃ nirvikalpo nirākāra rūpo
Vibhutvā ca sarvatra sarvendriyāṇaṃ
Na cāsaṅgataṃ naiva muktir na meyaḥ
Cidānandarūpaḥ śivo'ham śivo'ham

JOY CHAKRABORTY

Joy Chakraborty is an alumni of Ramakrishna Mission Vidyamandira, Belur Math. To imitate Vivekananda, he had taken the arduous task of tracing his footsteps - from the rarefied heights of Rishikesh to the samudra tirtha of Kanyakumari. He has written occasionally in e-magazines like Kritya and has even received a letter of appreciation from the British monarch Elizabeth II for his poetry. He founded the Vivek Vahini Volunteers, a society dedicated to social service, during the Covid19 pandemic. He now teaches English at Ramakrishna Mission Vidyapith, Deoghar. Ishaan is his first novel.